The Girl Who Lived on the Ferris Wheel

ALSO BY LOUISE MOERI

A Horse for X. Y. Z.
Star Mother's Youngest Child
How the Rabbit Stole the Moon

The Girl Who Lived on the Ferris Wheel

by LOUISE MOERI

E. P. DUTTON   NEW YORK

Library of Congress Cataloging in Publication Data

Moeri, Louise.   The girl who lived on the Ferris wheel.

SUMMARY: Til realizes with increasing urgency that her
divorced mother's violently abusive behavior is getting
more and more out of control.
[1. Child abuse—Fiction.
2. Mentally ill—Fiction]   I. Title
PZ7.M7214Gi   [Fic]   79-11359   ISBN: 0-525-30659-5

Published in the United States by E. P. Dutton, a Division
of Elsevier-Dutton Publishing Company, Inc., New York

Published simultaneously in Canada by Clarke,
Irwin & Company Limited, Toronto and Vancouver

Editor: Ann Durell   Designer: Stacie Rogoff

Printed in the U.S.A.   First Edition
10 9 8 7 6 5 4 3 2 1

to my son and his wife
Rodger and Barbara Moeri

1

It was bad enough to have a name like Clotilde (Til for short), she thought, squinting through the curtains at the empty, windswept street, but why did she also have to live part of her life in a bleak old tomb on Quesada Avenue in South San Francisco and the rest of it on a Ferris wheel at Playland?

It was Saturday morning again and she could almost feel the creaking, swaying seat of the Ferris wheel under her, the cold wind splashing against her legs, the up-back feeling of being sucked in by some great monster, the out-over lurch as she was again thrust out into space. But if she didn't go— didn't ride the Ferris wheel—it would mean staying home all day. And even the Ferris wheel was better than that. . . .

The clock had struck ten a minute ago and the early summer morning fog still blurred the San Francisco skyline to the north as Til chewed on her second piece of toast. She had put on a dark green wool skirt and white blouse, short socks and heavy saddle oxfords, and her blue corduroy jacket lay ready across a chair, but her hair was still uncombed. For some reason, although she knew that her father would appear at ten o'clock every Saturday (for the rest of her life, she supposed) to take her out for the day—she was never completely ready on time. Sometimes it was socks to be matched (or even darned), a belt to be located, a blouse to be ironed. Today it was hair. She laid the toast on the windowsill, raised the brush and started dragging it through her straight, dun-colored hair.

I wonder, she pondered, checking the street again, why I got straight, crummy, dishwater-colored hair, when both my parents have curly hair? Pop's is red and curly. Mom's is black and wavy. My hair is like moldy straw. Limp. Hangs around my face like cold spaghetti. I'm eleven years old and have a round face and buggy blue eyes and a goofy name and hair like cold spaghetti. Sometimes I feel like I was made out of leftovers. . . .

Til took another bite of toast—it was barely warm now— and went on brushing while she watched through the narrow gap between the curtains. Behind her the living room was still shadowy and cold. The faded brown couch and chairs, the cheap blond end tables and china lamps sat rigidly parallel with the walls, their positions determined by her mother's yardstick. The drab striped wallpaper, the flowered rug, were barely visible because at this hour the sun breaking through the fog made only a narrow bar of gold across the floor directly under the window. The rest of the long, narrow house was still dark, still quiet. Mom must be in the basement, putting clean clothes through the washing machine. . . .

Til glanced at the clock—it was getting late—and then back at the street. There was Pop now, right on time, just turning the corner onto Quesada Avenue, heading up the hill into the cold wind. His brown overcoat flapped open, showing the old-fashioned quilted silk vest he always wore, and the gold watch chain draped across his barrel-shaped stomach. Even at this distance Til could see the frizzy orange twists of hair sticking out from under his narrow black Homburg hat like clusters of wire springs, and the curly red beard that concealed the lower part of his face.

As far back as she could remember, Pop had never looked any different, and everybody had always said Til looked a lot like her father—stocky and short, ruddy-skinned, with a broad German face and blue eyes. She sometimes wondered how she would look when she grew up, because Pop looked like the fat half of a comedy team from the movies—the one who plays the violin and speaks with a German accent. But of course, that's exactly what he is, she thought: a fat violin-playing comedian with a German accent.

As she dragged her hairbrush through the last thicket of tangles, she looked sharply to see if he were carrying the violin case. Yes, there it was, black and shabby, dangling from his big red hand.

Til knew that the only chance Pop had to play his violin was on his day off—the day he spent with her. Because Pop was like everyone else in this year of war, this year of 1943—he worked six long, hard days and nearly always overtime on his job, and into the seventh day of the week he crowded all that was left of life. He had persuaded his employer to let him work Sundays because he felt that Saturday was the best day for him to spend with Til—he could take her shopping for school clothes or to the dentist or doctor, if need be, on a Saturday. Those were the things he knew Gertrude hated doing; and if there were no necessary errands to be taken care of, they could always spend the day at Playland at the Beach.

So on Saturdays, Pop washed his clothes in the leaky sink of the one-room "apartment" he had occupied since the divorce, bought groceries, mended his socks and sewed on buttons, and always came to take her out. In such a crowded day off there was no time left for his violin unless he brought it with him when he came to see Til.

Pop's one ambition, as far as she could tell, was to become good enough to play with a small chamber music group he had become acquainted with. That's why the squirrels of Golden Gate Park and the sea gulls of Ocean Beach had to listen to "Hora Staccato" and "The Flight of the Bumble Bee." What *they* thought of Pop's music, Til could not tell, but she liked it.

One of her favorites was a silly, romantic love song that went: *"Du, Du, liegst mir im Herzen, Du, Du, liegst mir im Sinn—"* but Pop was afraid to play it for fear someone would hear him and get suspicious. This was a time of war, and he understood that a fat red-haired fellow with a black Homburg hat and a German accent as thick as a slice of bratwurst would be ill-advised to sit around in a public place playing German love songs. He might as well put on a Prussian helmet and march down Market Street tootling *"Deutschland, Deutschland, über Alles—"* on a tuba.

"Well," said Til, with the question of the violin settled, "now I can listen to *Moonlight* Sonata while I eat my hot dog."

She could guess at the rest of the menu too. One of Pop's coat pockets sagged heavily, and she knew it must contain a package of Fig Newton cookies. Along with his violin, the rides at Playland, and certain pieces of music, Pop had a passion for Fig Newtons and he always carried a sack of them deep in the linty pockets of his overcoat. As a private little joke between them, Til called him Sigmund-the-Figmund, and Pop made out as if he thought the name was hilariously funny. He gave her birthday cards and Christmas presents signed with the name; they had some fun with it—almost enough to make Til like fig cookies. . . .

Til glanced at the clock; it was getting late. She brushed harder and chewed down another piece of toast. Better hurry. Pop was a fast walker, for all his bulk, and it wouldn't take him more than a few minutes to make it up the hill. Before long he would be at the place on the street where it split into upper and lower levels. Quesada Avenue was one of the many streets in San Francisco where conventional city planning had to give way to unconventional landscape. Laid out along the side of a steep hill, it had been paved in two strips, upper and lower, separated by a steeply sloping bank. Weeds, tall shrubbery, and a row of short, scraggly palm trees grew up wild and rough along the bank, completely hiding the ground and even obscuring the view from one level to the other, unless you were a bird perched on the top twig of one of the bushes, or a girl standing at a window overlooking the street.

When she was smaller, Til had often slipped out of the house while Mom and Pop were fighting and not paying any attention to her, and crossed the upper section of the street in front of the house, eased down over the edge of the bank, and hid herself away under cover of the thick tangle of shrubbery. It made a perfect refuge, and she had shared it gladly

5

with the various homeless dogs and stray cats who came there, as she did, for a time of peace and shelter. Even the constant cold wind that always blew in San Francisco was tempered a little here, and on rare warm days a tiny summer could be found flat against the soil where dead leaves carpeted the ground and smelled of resin and mold.

Now through the crisply starched curtains, Til could see her father plowing up the street just below the bank, crossing to the upper section. In a few minutes he would stomp up the front step and pound his huge red fist on the door. (At one time he would have had a key; now he knocked.)

"I suppose you're late as usual—Til! What is *that* on the windowsill?" Her mother had entered the room behind her, silent as always on her rubber-soled shoes, and before Til could grab the toast, she had it pinned down. "What are you doing! You brought *food* into the living room? What are you thinking of? How many times have I told you never to take food out of the kitchen?"

Til stared down at the piece of toast. The muscles of her stomach began to contract into the usual tight, hard knot. No, she thought. Oh, *no*—

"How I *try*"—Gertrude's voice rose and her deep-set eyes began to burn—"how I try to take care of things here!" Her face was long and narrow, and when she got mad it made Til think of a huge axe with a sharp blade standing over you, ready to strike. "Dirty, greasy toast!" Her voice rose as she snatched up the bread.

Til's face tightened into a blank wall as she stared up at the woman towering over her. Her mother's tall, bony frame was like a piece of machinery, angular and jerky, and her black hair pulled back tight and coiled into a bun looked like a

6

knob on the machine, especially with the two or three knitting needles she always wore sticking through the bun. Til wondered why her mother nearly always wore a couple of knitting needles in her hair. She really didn't do all that much knitting anymore, although she had made a few sweaters for the Red Cross to send to the bombed-out people in Britain or to American servicemen overseas. But once she started putting the needles in her hair, she just kept it up, as if she didn't feel dressed without them. . . .

Her mother's voice droned on, becoming more shrill with every passing second: "How I *try* to keep this house up! After all, I have to work and earn a living—support *you*— five days at the plant and half a day on Saturday at the hospital—" Her face was getting hard and white.

She grabbed Til's shoulder and shook her sharply as if to get her attention, although they stood so close together it would have been impossible to have missed a word. "And the shopping, the errands—since *he* left, I do it *all,* now! Nobody cares how hard I work—I'm just a slave! A slave! Nobody cares about *me*—" Her grasp on Til's shoulder shifted to the upper arm. She jerked Til back and forth, and Til clenched her teeth as the joint between arm and shoulder began to shriek. "And now here you are scattering dirt and trash all over the house! All I do is work, but you don't care! You go out and have a good time with your father, while I stay here and work—work—*work*—"

Til twisted away sharply and wrenched clear of the powerful hand. Her shoulder was throbbing. She threw the hairbrush down and clamped her free hand over her bruised arm.

"There! There!" screamed her mother. "That's right— throw the brush down! *You* don't care—I'm just a slave

7

here—pick up after you—wait on you! Little princess—yes, you think you're a little princess, don't you, just like your name!''

Til bent and grabbed the hairbrush, but Gertrude leaned over and seized her again, jerked her to her feet, and reaching far back brought the open palm of her huge hand down flat and stinging over the side of Til's face. ''Princess! Princess!'' she shrilled. ''You're the princess and I'm the slave.''

The slap was so powerful it knocked Til out of her grasp. Her mother reached out again but Til was on her feet and running. She grabbed her coat and was across the room, lunged for the door just as a thunderous pounding sounded on the outside.

Til wrenched the door open. There stood Pop on the doorstep, smiling and bobbing and waving his violin case, happy to see her, happy it was Saturday again.

''Til!'' he shouted. ''Baby! Princess! Come to Poppa!''

Til plunged through the door and into Pop's arms. As they danced around on the front porch in a crazy, silly, hopping dance, Gertrude Foerester slammed the door behind them with a crash that shook the boards under their feet.

2

Pop always walked fast down Quesada Avenue, shoulders hunched, his feet making hurried, sliding sounds on the steep sidewalk; but Til ran, making circles around him, giddy and dizzy, and yelling silly things: "Knock! Knock!" "Who's there?" (from Pop). "Tijuana!" "Tijuana, who?" "Tijuana take me out to Playland, today, Pop?"

They would clasp hands and run across the street, Til skimming the pavement like a swooping gull and Pop huffing along like a steam engine. Because, although they never said so, neither of them felt really safe until they turned the corner and were out of sight of the house. Not that Gertrude had ever followed them or tried to bring Til back after she had left the house for her Saturday with Pop.

Once Til was outside the door, she was like a game piece—lost to her mother and temporarily in another player's territory. But Til always knew she was there behind the curtains at the front window, sullenly staring after them, shaking her head, smoothing her hair (and touching the knitting needles gently, carefully), pursing her lips over teeth that jutted forward under her long nose.

Only when they had turned the corner would her mother go back to the kitchen, where she would get out her mops and brooms and scrub brushes, her O'Cedar oil and polishing cloths, her Bon Ami, ammonia, soap and hot water. And scrub the house down to its raw bones while Til was gone. As they turned the corner and the fragrance of the coconut processing plant down along Third Street whisked up to greet her nose, Til knew that when she got home that night, the house would be cold and damp and smell of ammonia and floor wax and starch. But it would probably also be quiet . . . like other houses? . . . for a while. . . .

Pop glanced over his shoulder. "The bus! It's coming!" He shifted into a heavy jog and Til lengthened her stride; she was at the bus stop, dancing from one foot to the other, long before he lumbered up. As the smoking, rattling old city bus ground to a halt, they jumped on and Pop dropped two jingling dimes into the hopper. Til staggered down the aisle. The bus never really stopped—you sprang in through the folded-back doors as it slowed down, tossed your coin into the metal basin, and careened down the aisle, grabbing at the seat handles for support as the driver threw in the clutch, stepped down on the gas, and roared off down the street as if in pursuit of a German panzer division.

Til braced her feet and looked around. The bus was already crowded (hardly anybody could drive his own car these days with gas rationing so tight), and she and Pop had to stand in the aisle as usual. But there was still room enough for her to be able to see most of the other passengers. Across from her was a group of East Indians; there were several shoppers, men in uniform, two plump Chinese ladies in black satin trousers and quilted jackets, and over there a family—a mother with two children wedged onto the seat beside her.

Silently Til watched the family. The baby boy on the seat beside his mother wriggled and waved his arms; every minute or two he dropped his teddy bear on the floor of the bus. With grunts and groans the mother scooped up the teddy bear each time, dusted it off, handed it back to the child. Til felt the sweat break out on her back as she watched the baby throw the teddy bear. Throwing things on the floor was dangerous—dangerous—didn't the child know that? But the woman said nothing—just kept on picking up the dusty, plush-covered toy and handing it back. . . .

"Hey, Pop"—Til shifted her nervous gaze away from the baby—"guess what—I got an A in English and we beat the sixth-grade team in baseball! I hit a homer—"

"A-a-a-ah!" Pop's fuzzy red eyebrows rose and he chuckled. "So—we have an athlete here—and a very smart girl—"

"That's why my arm hurts"—Til raised her arm and her mouth turned into a crooked line as the bruised muscles grated in her arm—"I threw the bat."

Pop's face sobered. He reached out a huge paw and gently touched her shoulder. Til winced.

"Being a baseball star takes a lot out of you—" she hurried on, "but then you have to sacrifice something if you want to be great! Look, Pop, there's a Liberty ship at the pier"—she changed the subject suddenly—"and another one. Two, three, four—all the piers are full this morning. Which one did you work on yesterday?"

Til jerked restlessly around, staring through the window of the bus as the long line of piers south of the Bay Bridge now

11

became visible through the clearing fog. Beyond the railroad tracks, the blocks of warehouses, ramps and loading zones between Third Street, on which the bus ran, and the long line of piers jutting out into the bay north of the China Basin, they could make out the heavy outlines of cargo ships, hear the foghorns and the stevedores' whistles.

"Over there," said Pop. "Pier 42. See her? She has two loading booms. There—you can see the winches bringing up a big crate now."

"What were you loading?" Til asked, even though she knew he wouldn't tell her. It was a kind of game between them—every Saturday she would try to trick Pop into telling her what his longshoring gang had loaded during the week, and each time he nimbly outwitted her. They both knew he would never reveal any important information, and they both enjoyed the wild stories he made up: "Ah—you wouldn't *believe,* Til! We are sending one million sewing machine bobbins on the *Rowallan Castle* posthaste to the South Pacific because the hula dancers need them to sew up the holes in their grass skirts!"

She knew of course that he made up the "war secrets" to tell her—usually at the top of his voice on a crowded bus— and that he had never laid eyes on any of the ships he named. He siphoned the names of ships out of his memory and the conversations among the stevedores; and when he described a submarine named *City of Dogpatch* doing undercover work looking for disloyal oysters, it was unlikely that anyone took him seriously. Never once did he let a piece of significant information fall; the fat comedian with the fiddle was a lot smarter than he looked.

12

3

The bus groaned and the floor rippled under their feet. The tall lady next to Til had just jabbed her elbow into the side of Til's face again when the bus driver rapped out, "Market Street!" They scrambled toward the front and out through the folding doors onto the crowded sidewalk.

"How about a doughnut?" asked Pop as he peered through the window of Foster's, a big coffee shop on the corner. Inside, early shoppers with paper bags and lumpy purses were shuffling to and fro, carrying tiny trays of coffee and doughnuts to eat at the tables, or empty cups and crumpled napkins to the clean-up area.

"And hot chocolate?"

"Yah! Hot chocolate too!"

Til always thought she couldn't eat another bite after she finished the cold soggy bowl of cornflakes and the burnt toast her mother put on the table every morning of her life, but somehow the bus trip to Market Street did wonders for her appetite. She never ate less than three or four doughnuts and two cups of hot chocolate.

They had a favorite table, a tiny one in the Third and Market Street corner of the shop, where they were practically on the sidewalk, with only a pane of glass between them and the hustling shoppers, the clanging streetcars, the slow grind of the traffic, and, always, the cold wind.

Now, as Til sank her teeth into the second chocolate doughnut, Pop asked the Saturday question: "So? And how has it been for you this week?"

And she gave the Saturday answer: "Oh . . . so-so. Same. *You* know—"

A big lump of chocolate-frosted doughnut stopped halfway down her throat and just hung there, like a stalled elevator. Til's eyes watered. Something like this always happened to her whenever Pop asked her the Saturday question. Sometimes she sneezed. Sometimes it was an itch, other times a coughing spell. If they were on the street, she stumbled; if they were on the bus, she was jostled off-balance. And always by the time she had recovered, Pop had nodded and the moment was past. And he never asked the question twice.

She wanted to answer differently: tell him, or somebody, about it. The trouble was—what *was* the trouble? What was there to say? That Mom was cranky, a nagger? He knew that—it was why he had moved out of the house. That Mom sometimes slapped her, pushed her around? Other parents did the same—there were kids who got punished much harder than she, for playing hooky, stealing out of dime stores, throwing rotten tomatoes at police cars. But not for eating toast in the living room. . . .

Til wished she could find a book or something that had a list of prescribed punishments for crimes: so much for leaving a ring in the bathtub, so much for losing your sweater, so much for being sassy. Then she could read it and decide whether or not—or how far—Mom was really off base. As it was, she couldn't be sure.

All I know, she sometimes thought, is how it is with me. Is it any different with other kids? What I can't figure out is: How bad is bad? My problem is—do I have a problem? Which way is up? Maybe this is the way it is. Maybe I really *do* bring it all on myself—Mom says I do. It's true I do things she tells me not to, even though I know she'll get mad. Sometimes . . . sometimes I wonder if I do them on purpose. . . . But then, a person probably *shouldn't* eat greasy toast in the living room—

And then . . . there was something else. It was just a little thing, a vague thing, a thing she felt rather than understood. Pop was . . . well, he was *Pop*. Fat. Funny. A fiddle player. Cracked jokes, made up stories to hear people laugh. Pop didn't go around looking for trouble. It wasn't that he wouldn't listen to her—it wasn't that he probably wouldn't help her (if he could)—but she knew for a certain hard mean fact that Pop's round face would cloud over, that he would back away, if she came to him with bad news, with a plea for help. She had always known that there was something in Pop that wouldn't stand too much pressure. Otherwise, why would he have left the house in the first place? No, it was better just to keep their Saturdays the way they were—happy, relaxed and silly—islands of sunshine to look forward to through the week.

"Yah." Pop nodded as his daughter answered the Saturday question.

He ate his doughnut the way she did, biting off big chunks and washing them down with gulps of hot coffee, as if someone might come along and take it away from him if he didn't hurry.

He had learned to eat that way, living with Til's mother. Gertrude was queer. She would fix a meal, and although it wasn't all that good, you had worked hard and you were hungry; you sat down to eat it. But almost immediately she would discover some reason why you must not eat that particular bit of food right now—it was too hot and must be allowed to cool, or you took too long to get to the table and it was cold—it must be taken to the stove to be reheated. She must remove it to skim off grease, add salt, stir it up, smooth out lumps.

If you dared to grab a few bites, it would touch off an explosion because here she was, working her fingers to the bone to put decent food on the table, and you didn't appreciate it. You had to be a gulper to get some of it down before she was at your elbow and her long skinny hands had pirated your meal, to take it back to the kitchen where she fiddled with it just long enough for you to lose all interest in eating it. At which point she would bring it back, set it down in front of you, and force you to eat it. And if you didn't eat it, a quarrel could start that would last for days. . . .

Helmut Foerester reached into his pockets for his pipe and tobacco, but then he sat with them in his hand, forgotten. Once again he felt the pleasant bustle of the coffee shop coming between him and Til and the Saturday question.

It was always the same. Every Saturday he made up his mind to find out how things were at home for Til—really ask

16

and get an answer—and then . . . and then Til would shrug her shoulders, would turn away, would cough or sneeze or change the subject somehow, and the moment would pass. He could see she didn't want to talk about it—nothing could be plainer.

But, he wondered, should he *make* her talk? What was there to talk about? He knew Gertrude was grim and gloomy and hard to live with—he had divorced her only when it was plain to him that she would never change and there was no other course open to him. If he had stayed with her, he would have become like her—he would have had to, to survive. Gertrude's irritability was like a disease that would spread if he wasn't careful, and soon he would have become just as unreasonable as she was—in different ways, maybe, but still unreasonable.

He was not a young man when he married Gertrude—in fact, both of them were past the time in life when most people married and had children—and perhaps that made them both less resilient, less patient and flexible. Sometimes he felt old and brittle, a man trying to fool everybody into thinking he was younger, stronger than he really was, but failing, failing, every day.

And nothing, as far as he could see, could be accomplished for himself or Til by letting Gertrude drive him under. So he had got out; but of course the court had awarded Til's custody to Gertrude. Minor children were always left in the custody of their mothers; he had known from the first that the most he could hope for was visitation rights. And that left him right where he sat now. All I can do is take her away from the house every Saturday. And love her. And buy her a ride on the Ferris wheel.

17

"Well," he said at last, "I guess we don't have any other choices. I know it's hard. . . ."

Til nodded. She was spinning a doughnut on her finger, nipping little bits out of it as it turned. Well, so much for the Saturday question; the time had come and gone again. She felt regret and relief at the same time. But how can I tell somebody something I don't understand and *he* doesn't understand? Some trick. So I guess I'll just eat fast, dodge when I see something coming, keep my mouth shut, and not let on that I'm afraid of the Ferris wheel. . . .

For Pop had never once guessed that the great, wobbling, wavering wheel terrified her so much that she dreamed about it—dreamed that she was locked forever behind the steel bar of the Ferris wheel seat, sentenced to spend her whole life going up—and—up—and—over, sick and dizzy and unable to escape. Round and round like the doughnut—

Til would have liked to stay downtown today with the shoppers, the crowds on Market Street, the kaleidoscope of color, sound, smell; but Pop never wanted to do that. Like most men (she supposed) he had no interest in window-shopping or strolling through the stores just to look. But there were a thousand things Til could have found to do downtown if Pop would agree.

They could go to Chinatown and look at the grocery stores, stare at the street signs in Chinese, wander through the curio shops jammed with imitation lacquer boxes, cheap pottery and bamboo knickknacks. She wanted to eat shrimp cocktail on Fisherman's Wharf, climb Coit Tower, ride the ferry across the bay and then take another ferry back, getting off at last, wind-whipped and chilled through, with a vision of white-capped waves to see at night inside your eyelids just before going to sleep. And she had always wanted to buy a candid snapshot taken by one of the sidewalk photographers who walked backwards among the crowds on Market Street. They took pictures of people as they hurried along, and then accosted their subjects with offers of exciting souvenir pictures at bargain prices. They took your money and your name and address, and a day or so later you would receive in the mail a blurry picture of yourself, mouth open and eyes squinted, dodging the glut of pedestrians on Market Street. Ugly, but they were fun.

But Pop thought the photographers were an abomination, and he threatened to hit them with his violin case. "Don't worry!" he cried to Til driving off a spidery little man in a yellow slicker who had just snapped her picture. "I'll get rid of him!" The photographer disappeared in the crowd, and so did Til's chance of receiving a picture of herself in a letter addressed to *her*.

On the pretext of needing pencils for school, she managed to drag Pop into Woolworths for a few minutes. Til's idea of heaven had always been to be able to buy one of anything she wanted in Woolworths; it would have taken a truck to carry it all home. None of the things she wanted cost much, but Pop couldn't give her much pocket money, and Gertrude gave her none at all, so a purchase had to be engineered with cunning and guile.

Til loitered as long as possible up and down the aisles, pretending she didn't know where the stationery counter was located. But Pop spotted it and hustled her over to it, and she was only able to stall for a moment over a choice between red, yellow, blue and green pencils. But along with the pencils, Pop bought her a red comb, a little pin in the shape of an American flag for her jacket, and a tiny three-ring notebook with leather-printed covers. The notebook was so small she would be able to carry it in her coat pocket and use it anywhere. A lucky afterthought struck her and she asked for a pencil sharpener—they found one shaped like an apple—and that, added to the pencils and notebook, would make it possible for her to pass notes all day at school. . . .

On Market Street again Pop began to watch the buses. "Let's see, this one? No. This one? No, not yet—" With his hand on her shoulder he guided her through the opposing currents of the crowd. Besides the up-and-down-the-sidewalk pedestrians, there were at every streetcar and bus zone some who bolted across the inside lane of pavement to stand, huddled and vulnerable, in the loading area until their car or bus came clanging and hissing along and scooped them up like someone in the movies being rescued from a cattle stampede. Til would have liked to take a ride on the cable cars today— she loved the rattling, clanging little trolleys that swooped up and down the hills with people clinging to them like ants, but they ran only on the steepest hills. Fulton Street, the way to Golden Gate Park (they often stopped there before going on to Playland), was nowhere near to being steep enough to need a cable car.

As they made their way up Market Street, Til, too, was watching the buses, on the theory that if you couldn't beat the Playland game, you might as well join it; and she almost missed a remarkable fact: she had lost Pop.

She turned abruptly to see what had happened, and her eyes bulged. There stood Pop dead still in the middle of the sidewalk, staring straight into the camera of a sidewalk photographer. And the man who chased photographers off with his violin case just stood there, feet spraddled, with a silly half-smile on his face, looking at the woman who held the camera.

Instantly and vaguely jealous, Til raked the woman with her eyes. How come he stopped for *her*? There was nothing pretty, however, or especially eye-catching about the photographer. She was almost as old as Pop, and wore a black leather coat and brown slacks. She had a white straw Panama hat on her head, with tiny printed business cards, a memo pad, and pencils sticking up out of the band like feathers in an Indian headdress. Her hair was blonde and curly (the kind *I'd* like to have, thought Til swiftly), and her broad red face under the blonde ringlets was crinkled and merry.

"Smile! Smile!" cried the photographer, raising her camera and quickly focusing on Pop and Til as Til dodged back to grab his hand. "Smile—that's good! A lovely picture of papa and daughter! And the address, please?"

The woman, who had a German accent like Pop's, reached up to her hat for the pad and a pencil, and Til, wondering why the heavens didn't fall, mumbled her name and the address of Quesada Avenue. At any moment she expected Pop to pick her up by the collar, shoulder the photographer into the gutter, and roar off down the street. But no, there he stood, still smiling, blinking, speechless, mild as a duck. In another moment he had handed the photographer some money, and the woman smiled again, waved, and slipped away to vanish in the crowd. Only then did Pop rouse himself and begin to move down the street.

Til followed, trailing after him in profound amazement. "Wow," she muttered. "I wonder how she did that. That's the first time I ever saw anybody make Sigmund-the-Figmund say *cheese*! Maybe it was her German accent."

4

They got off the bus at Golden Gate Park because Til, although she didn't say so, felt she wasn't up to facing the
Ferris wheel just yet. Maybe, if she could persuade Pop to
walk around through the Arboretum, the Steinhart Aquarium,
the De Young Museum, they could use up a couple of
hours—even more if they had a hot dog and a soda.

The park was crowded today, although over here on the
west side of Twin Peaks, the sun had not yet broken through
the fog, and the air was chill. Redwood and eucalyptus trees
sprinkled showers of icy water on anyone who brushed
against a low-hanging branch, and the rhododendrons dripped
what looked like colored diamonds from their brilliant petals.
The flower beds smelled wet and spicy, and back in the dells,
off the asphalt and gravel paths, the ground was so damp
your feet didn't make a sound. But then even with the people
sauntering up and down—tourists with cameras, servicemen
on leave, families on outings—the park always seemed
quieter when the fog was in. Days when the sun shone, it
was gay and noisy; Til liked the sunny days much better.

After they had walked silently past the Egyptian mummies,

the Indian artifacts, and the Louis XVI furniture in the De Young Museum, the stuffed birds and animals in the Museum of Natural History, and stared goggle-eyed at the fish (who stared goggle-eyed back at them) in Steinhart Aquarium, Til began to think of her stomach again.

"How about something to eat?" she asked, beginning to drift toward the snack bar. "And we haven't crossed the Moon Bridge yet today."

They threaded their way through the crowd, which was getting heavier all the time, and at last stood beside a little artificial stream, looking up at the utterly improbable structure of heavy planks that arched the water like a wooden rainbow. The Moon Bridge was nearly a complete circle, rising from each bank in such an arc that to climb it you had to be surefooted and agile, and have hands free to grasp the rails and pull yourself up and over. Pop rarely attempted it; he stood on one side, smoking his pipe, nodding and smiling, as Til scrambled from one side to the other.

Each time she stopped at the crest of the bridge to look down at the stream, at Pop, at the flowers, the Tea Garden beyond, as if to make sure it was all still there. Because the Moon Bridge was such an unlikely kind of bridge—it seemed to have been made for a different world, a different people. No one who simply wanted to cross a stream would build a Moon Bridge. A fallen tree trunk would get you across water, and you didn't need this wild, powerfully curving bridge that was actually so hard to climb that it hindered your progress across the stream more than it aided you. Odd people, the Japanese, she thought, to make what was supposed to be an easy passage, so difficult. . . .

"Odd," said Til, peering into her popcorn bag.

"What is *odd?*"

"Queer. Funny. Weird. But beautiful."

"Hah?"

"The Japanese." Til never said "the Japs," like most everyone else did these days. Pop had taught her not to.

"Hmmmm?" Pop was listening but his eyes signaled *Don't talk too loud.* With your country at war with Germany and Japan, it was not safe to be heard coming down easy on anything German or Japanese. Some people had stopped eating frankfurters; in Seattle a crowd had attacked and burned a shipment of Japanese *calendars.*

"Odd. The bridge—it's hard to understand why anybody would build a bridge so hard to walk over. Makes me think . . . ." she said absently, "of my name. . . ."

Pop's eyebrows rose. "Your name?" He had long ago told her the origin of her name. The first Clotilde had been a princess of Burgundy who—a Christian—married a ferocious pagan, Clovis, king of the Franks, and then in the year 496 led her husband to accept Christianity. Together Clovis and Clotilde became forerunners of the Christian rulers of Central Europe.

Helmut had selected the name of the princess for his own precious daughter—thinking he was doing his child a favor, giving her a pleasant fortune, as if the good fairy from some old story might one day visit her with gifts. But as it turned out later, the name was no favor to Til because Gertrude had planned to name the baby after herself, only Pop got there ahead of her and had his selection entered on the birth certificate while Gertrude was still groggy from the anesthesia of the delivery room. And when Gertrude found out that Clotilde was the name of a *princess,* it seemed to form the nucleus of the nervousness and irritability that took possession of her from that day on. She was like an oyster with a grain of sand under her shell, except that instead of producing a lovely pearl, the irritant produced anger and, very soon, jealousy.

Other people just thought *Clotilde* was an odd and unfamiliar name. By now Til had heard every possible variation and every possible joke that could be made out of it. That was why the name reminded her of the Moon Bridge: a name was supposed to help you identify yourself, make it easier to meet with other people, but *Clotilde* threw all kinds of obstacles in her way. It made her climb high and hard, and gave her a feeling sometimes of not belonging to either side of the stream. . . .

Playland was even colder than the park, and the fog streamed in over the low dunes of Ocean Beach. Til turned her collar up, blew on her icy fingers, and tried to think of excuses to stay off the Ferris wheel. Pop bought tickets for the roller coaster and they rode, and the wind was so cold Til felt that her face would freeze and fall off in pieces. She could picture how it would look: an eye, a nose, another eye, a mouth, lying here and there on the littered ground between the shabby concession stands. No doubt they would all be swept up without so much as a second glance by the team of old men who made feeble attempts to keep the litter—popcorn boxes, Popsicle sticks, soft drink bottles, gum and candy wrappers—from getting so deep that Playland disappeared completely under it.

They rode the bumper cars once, had a hot dog, and then

rode them again. This was Til's favorite ride, as Pop's was the Ferris wheel, and she was sure he hated the bumper cars as much as she hated the Ferris wheel. Pop had no killer instinct; once he had crumpled all his bulk into the tiny car, he was everybody's hit-and-run victim. Smiling hopefully, he would start timidly around the arena, only to be struck again and again as the other drivers steered their little electric vehicles past or at him. Pop spent the whole ride careening around like a Ping-Pong ball, bouncing off the walls and the other cars.

But not Til. When Til climbed into the little car, she turned into a cross between Barney Oldfield and King Kong. With clenched teeth and joy in her heart, she zoomed out into the arena and pursued, battered, and left spinning behind her every other car on the floor. Only when the electricity was turned off at the end of the ride and all the little cars roared to a halt did she turn back, like a changeling, into herself again.

But after Pop had taken two rides in the little cars, he had to calm his nerves with a ride on the Ferris wheel. Til had to admit that fair was fair, but she followed him numbly as he bought the tickets. They waited briefly in line, mounted the wooden platform, and were admitted by the attendant into one of the bright-colored swinging seats as the wheel paused for them.

The moment they were in the seat and the bar clanged shut in front of them, Til's stomach tied itself into a knot. Sweat broke out on her chest and back, making her feel colder than ever. While Pop relaxed and grinned and shouted: "Aha! Now we ride where they can't bump us!" Til stared down at the dirty ground and wanted to climb out and lie down and kiss it. Oh, to be down there with the cigarette butts, the crumpled candy wrappers, the Cracker Jack boxes, the half-eaten ice cream cones—

Then the motor roared, there was grinding and clanking, and the wheel trembled as if it felt a joyous tremor of rage upon finding that once again Til was in its power. (The Ferris wheel was so big—so big—and there was nothing you could do to stop it; the Ferris wheel could pick you up and throw you—maybe even kill you—and nobody—nobody—nobody—could stop it—)

The wheel began to turn, slowly and then faster, faster, and Til felt herself lifted up and flung backward as if someone, hating her, had struck her. All the blood in her body swooped into her feet and stayed there until they reached the top of the turn, and then it left her feet and splashed up into her head like water in a spinning bucket, only to return to her feet again on the next revolution of the wheel.

Sometimes, while riding the Ferris wheel, Til occupied herself by wondering why she hated it so much. It wasn't fast, not too noisy. No colder than any of the other rides. She had decided it must be the feeling of being thrown and threatened by something so much bigger and stronger than herself that made her hate it so much—the feeling that she no longer had control of her body or her life. But then all the rides except the bumper cars did pretty much the same thing to you, didn't they? Nevertheless, the Ferris wheel was the one she saw turning and turning against the black screen of her eyelids just before she went to sleep at night. Every night. . . .

They decided to walk on the beach for a few minutes before they caught the bus back to Market Street. Now, late in the afternoon, the sky was clearing briefly and the sunlight glowed on the offshore fog. Gulls wheeled in over the beach, screaming, and the surf broke with a thundering green roar a few yards to their right as they walked down the wet, hard-packed sand beyond the seawall.

Til took a handful of Fig Newtons out of the sack in Pop's pocket and munched them as they walked. The crumbs that dropped were immediately seized by the gulls who seemed to be able to see them from high in the air. Her face was spattered with salt spray, and with a cookie clenched between her teeth, Til had to borrow Pop's handkerchief to wipe it clean. Pop was very quiet; he walked slowly, staring out into the silvery haze of the fog, and his crisp curly hair vibrated like copper wires in the wind.

Til reached out to touch the violin case in Pop's hand. He had carried it all day as a woman would carry a baby or a child would carry a doll.

"You haven't played any music yet," she cried above the roar of the surf and the wind.

Pop nodded. He looked lonely.

"I know! Let's go sit there behind that big bunch of rocks at the end of the beach, and you can play me a song." Til grabbed his arm.

Pop's face was bleak. "No place here for music," he muttered. The wind was whipping his coat and hat and throwing piles of foam up at the edge of the waves.

"Sure there is!" cried Til. She raced ahead, checked out the rocks, ran back to Pop, took his hand, and hustled him forward into the shelter.

It was just a jumble of boulders, pounded and broken by the sea, that now at low tide were above the line of surf and

29

so relatively dry. Behind the rocks, on the landward side, it was somewhat sheltered from the wind, but still cold and incredibly noisy.

"Play 'Traümerei,' " she said, as she peeled some seaweed off the rock so Pop could sit down. "I like that one."

Slowly Pop sat down, opened the case, took out his violin. But he sat in silence, motionless, for such a long time that Til began to wonder if he had forgotten the music. She hummed a few bars as she watched him, waiting. Pop's hands, holding the violin and bow, were scarred and rough; she wondered how he managed to work as a stevedore and still keep his hands from being ruined for the violin.

Impulsively she reached out and smoothed her own hand over his. "I hope nothing ever happens—" she began, and then stopped.

"Hah? What do you think—something to happen?" he asked, rousing himself.

"Your music. I hope nothing ever happens to spoil your music."

"Oh . . . just a little fiddle-scraping. . . ." Pop tried a smile, but Til could see it was forced. "Just a few little tunes on a fiddle—"

"But—that's all the music we have," said Til.

Pop's head snapped up and he met her gaze full on; it was like looking at blazing blue lanterns, Til thought, almost drawing back. I didn't know Pop's eyes could shine so bright—

Then he began to play.

She could see that he was shaking with the cold and his fingers were stiff, but for some reason Til had never heard his music sound better.

30

Pop played half a dozen songs, one after the other. Til sat in silence, staring at him. He seemed to be playing for a glittering audience instead of sitting there wrapped in his old coat (she suddenly could not remember his ever having any other coat) playing music on a cold, darkening beach where each wave came inches higher on the sand, and then fell back leaving a curving line of cream-colored bubbles to pop and disappear.

Why are we here? All at once the question rose up and surrounded Til, blotting out the rocks and the sand and the wind—even Pop's music. Why are we out here? We ought to be sitting in our own house, our own living room, with Pop playing and me listening, with Mom making hot chocolate in the kitchen. That's how it ought to be. What are we doing out here on the beach at sunset—him playing his violin in the cold wind and me sitting here on this wet sand listening? Why *are* we here—

At last Pop lowered his violin, took out the old flannel shirt that he kept it wrapped in, and laid it back in the case. He put the bow under its keeper and shut the lid. "Time to go," he said.

Til nodded. She scrambled up and brushed the sand off her skirt and socks. Together they started back across the beach toward the stairway in the seawall.

Another Saturday was almost over.

5

Sunday came up cold and bleak. Til awoke early but decided to stay in bed as long as she could, wishing her mother would allow more heat in the house.

Gertrude seemed not to notice either cold or heat very much, and if she did, it was to take exception to whatever others felt. If you were cold, she said it was really quite warm. If you were too hot, she closed the window and turned the heater up.

Til pulled the blankets over her head and was just well asleep again when the door of the bedroom burst open and slammed against the wall. The floor trembled as Gertrude strode across the room, bumping heavily against the side of the bed. She reached down and grabbed the blankets and ripped them back.

Til reared up, gasping in the chill, blinking, barely awake.

"Get out of that bed!" shouted her mother. "I've got to wash the sheets!"

"You just—washed them—yesterday—" stammered Til.

Her mother reached beyond her and grabbed the corner of

the bottom sheet, yanking it so fiercely that it jammed under Til's body. Til scrambled sideways, but not fast enough. Before she could get off of it, there was a ripping sound and the sheet split down the middle.

Til hit the floor running and headed for the door, but she was not completely awake and not nearly fast enough. Gertrude caught her easily and yanked her up short.

They stood in tense silence, Gertrude bending over her like a bad-smelling monster. I wonder why she always smells bad, thought Til, just before Gertrude's palm came down across her face.

The force of the blow broke her loose from her mother's grasp. It always did. It was like a dropkick: Gertrude would hold her out and then hit her, and the blow would throw her across the room. It was like being turned into a football and played with, but this game had only one player.

Til struck the wall, careened off, made it out the door and downstairs to the bathroom. She slammed the door and locked it. For a moment she rested her head against the door, and then stepped back. She slid the thick, warm bath mat over against the door and sat down on it, after pulling an extra towel out of the cabinet to wrap around her shoulders. For several moments she sat looking around the tiny room, with its old style plumbing, the roll of tissue on the holder, the stacks of soap and towels visible through the half-open door of the cabinet. It looked sane and normal and safe—

"—for today," she heard herself say. "That's all for today—"

She knew her mother would not hit her again today. One-a-day, like the vitamins. That was the rule. One a day. Actually, it would probably be a fairly nice day. . . .

The small window on the west side of the attic was full of cobwebs and streaked with dust. Til sat with her back against the glass even though it was very cold, and stared around at the piled boxes and barrels. Times like these, with Gertrude busy in the basement or out scrubbing the front walk, Til liked to slip away up to the attic. This was the only part of the house that Gertrude did not constantly scrub and polish, because she was afraid to climb the very steep flight of stairs in the back hall that led up to the trapdoor in the ceiling. The contrast between the cluttered, dusty attic and the antiseptically clean lower rooms was startling; but that was not the only reason Til came up here.

Gertrude had a strange habit. Left to herself, she would soon dispose of anything Til or Helmut—when he still lived there—had owned, unless it was actually being worn or held in their hands. She would invent all kinds of reasons why this or that object must go: it took up too much room, it was dirty, noisy, ugly, useless.

As the years passed, all of Til's old toys and games had disappeared until there was nothing left now. Other kids her age had dolls, games, penny banks, roller skates, balls, shelves of dog-eared books that they could look at and say, "I've had this since I was a baby." But all of Til's childhood possessions were gone—relentlessly thrown into the garbage or the incinerator by Gertrude when she was engaged in her endless "cleaning."

Sometimes when she tried very hard, Til could remember

some dolls, a wicker carriage, a teddy bear, a puppet or two, a book of Mother Goose rhymes. But they had all been gone for years now, and there was not so much as a single object left in the house or in her room to recall her babyhood. Sometimes she doubted that she had ever been a baby (there were no snapshots or photos—Gertrude hated them) or even a small child.

She could not remember such a time—or any long-distant past—so perhaps she had just started living a few years ago, appearing suddenly in the world as a child old enough to start school. One part of her mind knew that this was not true, and that she was truly the child of her parents and had been born and brought to this house and no doubt wore bibs and diapers and cried and ate and grew. But then another part of her mind would say, "How can I be sure? There's nothing of me here except what I'm wearing right now. Even my last summer's tennis shoes are gone. Maybe there *was* no last summer— maybe no last year—maybe I just made them up—"

The lack of old things that belonged to her had disturbed Til for a long time, although she was careful never to mention it to Gertrude. For as long as Til could remember, conversation with Gertrude had been reduced to the bare bones of essential questions and answers, and even then you couldn't count on getting an answer to a question as simple as When's dinner? Gertrude often took such inquiries as if they were invasions of her private right to conceal facts, and they would easily result in no dinner at all. . . .

But one day a year or so back, some vague impulse had sent Til to explore the attic. At first she had had some hazy idea that she might find a mysterious dusty paper that would reveal her to be the child of royalty—spirited out of some far-off kingdom—or at the very least an adopted child. Nothing of that kind ever turned up, however, so she was reluctantly forced to conclude that she was truly Gertrude's natural child.

But there were other things in the attic that turned out to be valuable—probably in the end more valuable than proof she was an orphan. For the attic contained her own real lost beginnings. There was a box of watercolors, partly used, with a fuzzy brush and a set of little pans for mixing colors. Helmut had given them to her years ago, and Gertrude had immediately pounced on them and declared they were "dirty." Pop must have put them up here to keep Gertrude from throwing them out, and then forgot about them.

Over here in this old trunk were a tiny dress and some bonnets—baby clothes. Til put her fingers through the sleeves of the dress, tried the bonnets on her fist. And even though she could not, of course, remember them, she knew she had once worn them, had indeed been a baby like other children.

There were a few other things—a set of checkers, a child's little painted wooden chair, part of a doll's quilt with lambs appliquéd on it, a heavy china bowl that had a picture of Goldilocks and the three bears painted on the inside. Although she had searched the whole attic carefully, Til never found anything beyond these few objects, and after a long time she had gathered them all together in a box which she set by the west window. Then once in a while she would slip up the attic stairs when Gertrude was busy or gone, and sit there and look at them.

She had just placed them all back in their box now—it was time to go back down the narrow, steep stairs—when a sound from outside the house caught her ear. First there was a wavering cry, then a harsh squawk. A cry, a squawk. A cry, a squawk.

Til fitted the lid on the box and turned to look out the window.

Opposite and below her was the east side of the house next door and the narrow yard that surrounded it. The house belonged to old Mrs. Fundy, a widow of considerable age, who had lived there as long as Til could remember. Mrs. Fundy was nearly deaf, a gentle, befuddled old lady, who had only the vaguest idea of what was going on and rarely ventured out of doors.

Til, knowing how impossible it was to talk to the deaf woman, would only smile and wave if she happened to see her. She was more interested in the old lady's parrot, a huge, moth-eaten old bird that lived in a big wire cage kept in an otherwise empty back bedroom. The parrot's name was Hibiscus, and his feathers were soiled and rather worn looking, as if he needed a new suit of clothes and his mistress was too poor to buy him one. He lived an easy life; having a deaf mistress, he had never even been required to talk, and he spent his days eating sunflower seeds, splattering droppings on the newspapers under his perch, and watching for opportunities to slip out of his cage.

Now from her high vantage point in the attic window, Til looked down upon a remarkable sight. The back door of Mrs. Fundy's house stood open, and through it Til could see the parrot's wire cage. The little door was open and the cage was empty.

Having absorbed that fact, Til turned to look at the yard that surrounded the old house. It had all been planted in

37

shrubbery so there would be no lawn to mow, and the bushes had grown up like a maze. There were little narrow paths threading here and there, and now Til saw that Mrs. Fundy was trudging up one path and down another. From time to time she let out a shrill little cry: "Hibiscus! Hibiscus! Where are you, Hibiscus?" Each cry was acknowledged by a hoarse croak, but as Mrs. Fundy was deaf, she could not hear the answers.

As Til watched, Mrs. Fundy came into view, tottering along and peering ahead down the serpentine path. And as she made her turn, Til saw, hobbling along behind her, the parrot, Hibiscus, who was plainly irritated by his inability to catch up with Mrs. Fundy or attract her attention. Hibiscus never flew—Til doubted that those ragged wings could lift him anymore—and he had probably got tired of being out in the cold, windy yard in a hurry. Now all he wanted was for his mistress to turn around and find him at her heels, and take him back into the warm house and feed him a cup of sunflower seeds.

Til giggled. She scurried quickly and very quietly across the attic, lifted the trapdoor and slipped down the stairs. In the kitchen she listened for a moment, but there was no sign of Gertrude anywhere. She let herself out the back door, ran down the walk between the houses, and scrambled to the top of the retaining wall. In a moment she had run around the path to a point where she could meet Mrs. Fundy head on.

Mrs. Fundy rounded the corner, still broadcasting her appeal: "Hibiscus! Hibiscus! Where are you, Hibiscus?" She halted in surprise when she saw Til, who was giggling and hopping around on the path. Til dove past the wobbly old lady, grabbed up the cranky parrot, who made a threatening swipe at her with his curved beak, and hauled him up to Mrs. Fundy.

Mrs. Fundy's wrinkled old corduroy face burst into concentric rings of smiles that spread from the roots of her white hair clear down into the collar of her dress. She bobbed and capered and laughed hugely, hugging the bedraggled parrot till his glassy yellow eyes bulged.

Til smiled and patted the parrot's tail feathers. She had known exactly how the frustrated old bird felt, and was happy now to see him cradled in safety. There was no use to try to talk to Mrs. Fundy—she couldn't hear a single word—so Til made some general, friendly motions, smiled, nodded, blew some kisses, and stood out of the way so the old lady could take her pet and go back into the house. Mrs. Fundy smiled and nodded and waved back at Til from the doorstep before she and the bird disappeared together into the house.

For another moment Til stood alone in the weedy, overgrown yard. Funny, she thought, Mrs. Fundy is deaf and Hibiscus is just a parrot, but whenever I come over here I feel like I've had a real *visit*—with *friends*—''

The basement was cold and very dark, but to Gertrude it was the best room in the house. Right from the beginning she had made it clear that the basement was hers, even though the others, Helmut and Til, insisted on occupying the other rooms upstairs. But of course she had not been able to stand that for very long, and little by little she had let them know that the upstairs was hers too. Actually, by right, Gertrude thought, it was all hers—the house, the furniture, the dishes, rugs, flowers in the yard—and had been, right from the start.

Because there was such a thing as justice, after all, and it had been completely plain to her from the first day they moved in that this house was to shelter and protect and hide Gertrude from a cruel and killing world out there. After all, she had waited all her life to have this house. Ever since she could remember, she had been forced to live exposed and unwanted (never, never being first and prized and petted) out in the hard middle of other people's rooms.

Her parents had not cared about her, protected her, loved her. In their house she had been only an ugly, awkward encumbrance, a kind of servant who waited on everybody. When she left home and went to work, it was the same thing all over—she worked in a restaurant and waited on people again, just like a slave. When Helmut came along and asked her, in his silly way, to marry him, she had quickly realized that it was the only chance she would ever have to find and keep a place of her own—a place where *she* would come first always.

But oh, how hard it had been. From the very first Helmut and Til kept trying to take it away from her—kept trying to take possession of bits and pieces of it, sometimes even whole rooms. It was like they were trying to take her very skin away from her, and thrust their own arms and legs into it, fasten it around them, leaving her exposed and dying in the cold.

Well, they weren't going to do it. She would never let them do it. Helmut was gone now, almost entirely, although he did come back on Saturdays (but not in the house—she never let him come into the house) and she was glad of that. Because he had never understood about the house. Helmut had never understood that the house had to be fixed and decorated and repaired and cleaned—cleaned—cleaned—

because it was her skin, her fleshly coat and dress that protected her from the cold, shielded her from outsiders. Helmut had thought the house was just pieces of wood and glass and brick; he could not see that it was her skin. Well, Helmut was gone now (as he should be) and she was left alone to take care of the house in the proper way. She worked to pay the mortgage; and then on the hours when she was at home, she cleaned and swept and mopped and polished it until there wasn't so much as a smudge or a crumb on her house-skin. If only Til—

About Til there was confusion in her mind. Sometimes when she was feeling particularly good—days when she was not aggravated or upset by something Til had done—she felt gentle toward Til. Til was, after all, her daughter, and everybody knew that a mother loved her daughter. Gertrude felt that she probably did, or if she did not now love her, then no doubt she would someday. But right now Til caused so much *trouble*. All over the house there were places where Til caused trouble, and often this trouble—quite naturally and justifiably—made Gertrude angry.

What else could it do, when she worked herself nearly to death trying to take care of the house? Why wouldn't it make her angry to see the throw rugs rumpled, a dirty glass in the sink, a washcloth hanging crooked on its rod? She worked as hard as she could to clean it all up and teach Til not to do these things, but lately it seemed as if it was all getting ahead of her, that no matter how hard she struggled, Til could always make more trouble.

Gertrude had redoubled her efforts, but in spite of it all there were still signs of Til everywhere—water splashes in the sink, a half-closed closet door, a cracker crumb beside a cupboard. Lately she had taken to washing the sheets on Til's bed every day so it would look as if no one ever slept there. Gertrude loved the sight of an immaculate bed, a clean, empty room. It was like putting on a silk dress that whispered smoothly over her skin to walk into a room that was clean, clean, clean, and had no sign of anyone ever having been in it.

A lot of trouble (and confusion) about Til, Gertrude felt, resulted from her name. It was the name of a princess, and when Helmut gave it to her (behind Gertrude's back, of course) he *made* her a princess, set her above Gertrude, who should always and ever have come first everywhere. How could it be otherwise? But here was Til who thought she was a princess, acted like a princess, oppressed and tyrannized others like a princess. It was intolerable. Sometimes—most times—when she thought about it, Gertrude's head ached and then her stomach got tight and sometimes she—

Sometimes she had to work very hard to beat Til down, make her accept her place, her rightful place. Gertrude looked down at her hands. They were clenched and sweating. Oh, no. I mustn't let myself think about Til, get upset. Think about something nice. Think about the basement—

Behind her the washing machine rumbled and surged as Gertrude began to walk about the basement, touching things now and then with one finger. Here were the fruit jars, all empty and washed, packed in boxes and then wrapped in brown paper and tied with string. From time to time she took the old paper off and put on fresh, just to be sure it was clean. Til had laughed at her for changing the papers on the boxes—said it was foolish. Gertrude had punished her for that, of course. She had a vague memory of blood running

42

down Til's face—she had hit her with the rake handle—and a feeling of regret that it was so very hard to teach Til anything at all.

Gertrude moved on to another part of the basement. Over on this shelf were the cans of paint. She was especially proud of these. They had once looked terrible, with awful dribbles of blue and green and pink paint down over their paper labels. She had been at wit's end trying to clean them up till at last it occurred to her to take all the labels off. Then, stripped down to a shiny silvery metal, each can was dusted every day. Gertrude beamed with pride at how they shone in the dusky light of the basement. She no longer knew, of course, which can held blue and which one pink, but that didn't matter. They were *clean*. A long time ago Til had wanted some paint for her bedroom—imagine that—but Gertrude put a stop to that in a hurry. It was just like Til, of course, always demanding, demanding, demanding—nothing was ever good enough for someone who thought she was a princess. . . .

Gertrude paused at the bin that held the old newspapers. About the old newspapers she had had many a bad moment. They were so awkward to wrap in the heavy brown paper, slipping and sliding around, but she had kept at it, each week adding another package tied with string and marked with the date. At one time there had been a few magazines in the bin, but their package didn't fit with the packages of newspaper; so she carried it down to the waterfront one day and threw it into the bay. After that she didn't buy any more magazines. There was no time to read them anyway, with her jobs and the housecleaning to do. Not that she read the newspaper either—hadn't read it in years. (And of course she had had to teach Til to leave it alone—a simple matter of striking her on the knuckles with a stick.) But it gave Gertrude a nice feeling each Sunday morning to wrap the brown paper and string around the last week's papers. It almost made her feel like she was going to church, observing a ritual, to wrap the week's papers and add them to the bin. . . .

There, the sheets should be washed enough by now. It took a lot of scrubbing to get all Til's dirt out. Now to rinse them and hang them out. Then she would scrub the sidewalks, clean out all the kitchen cupboards, mop and wax the kitchen floor, wash the ceiling. Hadn't been done for at least three or four days, and it must be filthy—

Gertrude sighed. If only Til just wouldn't cause so much trouble— Gertrude was reaching the point where she just couldn't stand much more of Til's troublemaking. . . .

Til sat in the cold living room hunched over the radio. It was small and cheap and had a tinny, squeaky tone, but it was a radio; and if the house ever caught on fire, it would be the first thing Til saved. The *only* thing, in fact. . . .

The windowpane on the west side of the room was streaming. The fog had cleared, only to be followed during the afternoon by rain, and the trickles of water made Til think of the beach yesterday and the green waves foaming over like waterfalls, the music of the violin, the hot chocolate she had wanted.

". . . Chocolate."

"What did you say?"

Til started. Gertrude had come up suddenly and silently in the doorway. In the near darkness Til had not seen her.

"Chocolate," said Til uncertainly. "I was thinking—

about hot chocolate. Could we—don't you—would some hot chocolate—be nice?''

"Hot chocolate!" her mother shouted. "Hot chocolate! If you think I'm going to drag out all that stuff—milk and sugar and cocoa—and get every pan and dish and spoon in the house dirty—spend another two hours on my feet—just a slave! You think I'm just your *slave*—!''

Til snapped off the radio. "I have to go to the bathroom," she said hurriedly.

In the bathroom she closed the very heavy old door and slid the bolt across. She kicked the bath mat over to the floor beside the door, pulled a dry towel off the rack and wrapped it around her shoulders, and folded her knees. As she sank down on the bath mat, her back to the door, she said to herself (reading from the society page of the San Francisco *Examiner*), "And here we show lovely Princess Clotilde sitting beside the pool at her palatial home on Quesada Avenue—"

—getting smaller. The world is getting smaller—smaller—smaller— When I'm not on the Ferris wheel, I'm locked in the bathroom. How much smaller can the world get—?

6

It was still raining on Monday, and Til put on her raincoat and hat. She rode the bus to school with dozens of other kids all dressed the same way and peering out from under floppy hat brims that dripped water down the backs of their necks. As a rule Til didn't mind rain (if you lived in San Francisco, rain was like an occupational disease, or the local werewolf), but today for some reason it made her unusually restless.

Instead of going inside the school building, Til drifted across the playground toward a group of girls huddled near the drinking fountains. Her best friend, Beverly, was there, sitting on her lunch box. Several other girls stood in a concentrated circle around her.

"What's the matter?" asked Til, peering at Beverly. Beverly was holding something in her hand—a shapeless blob of metal that looked like a specimen of fungus with sprangly arms and a blotchy, silver color. "What's that?"

"A piece of shrapnel. My father sent it home."

"Where'd he get it?"

"Out of his leg," said Beverly. She was sitting up proud

and tall on her lunch box. "His plane took some flak and he was wounded, and when they operated on him and took it out, he sent it home to us." Beverly's flat, round face beamed, and she held the ugly piece of metal as if she had just chipped it off the British royal crown.

Til wished scaldingly that she, too, had a piece of shrapnel and someone whose leg had been wounded. Beverly would attract admiring crowds all day. There were even a few boys who came up to see it, although all of them, or course, insisted that their fathers or brothers had been wounded long since with much larger pieces of shrapnel.

A gust of wind and rain swept across the playground, and quite a few people went inside. Beverly continued to sit on her lunch box holding court, and Til stood beside her now as the crowd thinned out. She would have liked to hold the shrapnel and feel its strange, hard lumps and knobs, but she was sure Beverly would never let it out of her hand. Beverly liked to talk about her father—he was a bombardier somewhere in Europe—and this would keep her going for days.

"—Don't really know how many missions he's flown," Beverly was saying now, "but we know it's a lot. He's going to write a book about his experiences after the war is over. My mother says—"

Til glanced from the shrapnel to Beverly's flat face, the round blue eyes. If the conversation was going to get around to mothers—

"My mother says when the war is over she wants to go to Europe to see where my dad was during the fighting."

"Hey, Bev," said Til tentatively, "about your mother—"

"My mother is a nurse, you know. She says it's the least

we can do to help the war effort while my father is overseas—"

"Your mother—your mom—hey, Bev, does she—does she ever—"

"My mother put herself through nursing school and graduated after my dad left with straight A's."

"Yeah? But, Bev, does she ever—I mean—when you do . . . something . . . you know, get in trouble at home—does—"

"I never get in trouble at home."

"Never?"

"Of course not. When I get home from school I have my snack and then do my homework, and then when she gets home from the hospital we fix dinner together for all of us—my brother's in high school, you know—and then we take turns doing the dishes. Mom tells us things that happened at the hospital and we tell her things that happened at school. On weekends we divide up all the big chores. Mom says if everybody pitches in, we can keep things going so Dad will be proud of us when he comes home. What's there to get in trouble about?"

"Well . . . she . . . I mean, your mother doesn't . . ."

"Doesn't *what*?"

"Well, that is . . . does your mother ever . . . punish you?"

"Whatever for? I don't do anything. Oh, if I get a bad grade on a quiz in math she sits down and shows me what I did wrong, or if my bed isn't made smooth she has me do it over. But I don't do anything to be *punished* for."

The warning bell clanged out over the playground and Beverly rose. She tucked the shrapnel into her coat pocket and picked up her lunch box. *Smug,* Til decided, was the word for Beverly, as she trailed bleakly after the confidently straight figure.

"But—hey—" she tried once more, a last time. *"If* you did something wrong—and *if* she punished you—"

"Yes?"

"Would she—do you think—she'd—*hit* you?"

Beverly stopped, turned to look at Til over her shoulder. "Of course not. What do you think my mother is—some kind of a *nut?*"

After the nine o'clock bell had rung and they were confined in the classroom, Til began earlier than ordinary to run through her repertoire of excuses for moving around. Her pencil lead broke and had to be sharpened; she had to throw away a spoiled sheet of paper; she did not understand this question. By the time she had made her third trip to the teacher's desk, she was so nervous her hands were shaking and she kept dropping things and bumping into furniture. Old Potato Face (Mrs. Hoogendorn, fifth-grade homeroom 222, Sir Francis Drake School's finest) stared up at her across a desk littered with arithmetic papers.

"Is anything wrong, Clotilde?"

"This problem—" Til stammered. "I can't seem to—I don't understand—I've gone through all the steps—"

Mrs. Hoogendorn reached out a large pink hand and took Til's paper. It was smudged, wrinkled, covered with figures that didn't go together, wrong answers, frenzied *X*'s that tried to obliterate mistakes. At the bottom of the page was a round face drawn in pencil with a huge open mouth and squinty eyes. The face said "Help! Help! I need help!" in a balloon.

Mrs. Hoogendorn stared for a moment at the paper. "Is *this* all you got done in a whole hour?" she said sadly.

Til nodded. Her fingers were drumming on the edge of Mrs. Hoogendorn's desk, and with her toe she was nudging the wastebasket back and forth over the floor.

Mrs. Hoogendorn took up her red pencil and tried to find a place to start a new problem, but the paper was so covered with disjointed attempts that she laid it aside and took a fresh sheet from her own desk. "Here"—she laid out a neat row of numbers—"and here. Now, the extraction of square root is basically a very simple process. —Clotilde, are you listening?"

"I'm listening!" Til's eyes snapped back to Mrs. Hoogendorn's face, away from the window at the far end of the room.

"First you must make a trial, in your mind, of what looks *reasonable*. Does nine go into two? No, of course not. Then does nine go into twenty-seven—?" She paused and looked up, waiting for Til to make the automatic response. But Til was looking at the globe on Mrs. Hoogendorn's desk.

"How—how far are we from—J-Japan?" Til asked suddenly. "Is it—very far?" For some reason her voice was jerky this morning.

Mrs. Hoogendorn stared at her quietly. She laid down the red pencil. "We are a long, long way from Japan. If you are afraid of being attacked by submarines or a bombing raid here in San Francisco, so far as I know there is no immediate danger. We are extremely fortunate in that regard. Other parts of the world, it's true, are suffering greatly. But not us—not right now. Clotilde, is your father in the service?"

"No—no—my—pop—is a—stevedore—"

50

"Ah. You have a brother in the service?"

"No—oh, no. No—brother. I'm alone—nobody—all *alone*—" Alone. Alone. She meant that she had no brothers or sisters. It came out kind of funny, but probably Mrs. Hoogendorn knew what she meant. "Alone. Alone."

Mrs. Hoogendorn rubbed a hand over her eyes. She was an elderly woman still teaching, because of the wartime shortage of teachers, when she should have been retired, with nothing more demanding to do than paste up her scrapbooks and spoil her grandchildren. Now her head was beginning to ache. She looked down at Til's paper again. Then she rose.

"Clotilde, I'm going to take you to see the school nurse. Class, I will be out of the room for a few moments. I trust you to take care of yourselves and maintain proper discipline. Everet Mosby, you will be paper monitor until I get back. Clotilde, come with me."

Til followed Mrs. Hoogendorn down the dimly lit hall. She had brightened a little. Any activity was better than trying to sit still and think about square roots. The trouble was, she was absolutely not sick. No sore throat. No fever. No ache. She didn't even have a skinned knee. Anxious to parlay this unusual stroke of luck into a couple of hours out of the classroom, she tried to drum up an illness, but nothing whatever came to mind. She had just decided on an upset stomach (safe, reliable, and no external symptoms) when they arrived at the nurse's office and Mrs. Hoogendorn directed her to a chair.

Then Mrs. Hoogendorn and Mrs. Foley, the nurse, went into a huddle at the back of the room beside a white cabinet with a Red Cross first-aid insignia painted on the side. Til

51

could hear them whispering but couldn't make out any of it. Since she had not asked to be brought here, she had a clear conscience, but she thought she ought to look sick, just in case. She sighed and tried to lean her head on her hand, but was unable to sit still even long enough to appear ill. Her head jerked up, she twisted back and forth. Her hands turned into fists that drummed on the wooden frame of the chair.

The conference had ended and the school nurse approached her.

"Clotilde, how are you feeling this morning?"

Til blinked. "Well," she mumbled, "my stomach—ah—well, it's—kind of—*icky*—"

"Icky?"

"Not—I mean—you know—it feels—"

"Like you might vomit?"

"Uh—yes. Like when you—ride—the Ferris wheel—"

The two women looked at each other. Not many people complained of motion sickness resulting from riding a Ferris wheel. A merry-go-round maybe, roller coaster certainly, but—a Ferris wheel? And on *Monday* morning?

"Tell me about it," said the nurse.

"Ferris wheel—" said Til, wondering where this line of discussion was going to take her. "It—ah, throws you—around and around, you know. Up—and—down. Back and forth. Throws you—over and over—"

The nurse was frowning. Mrs. Hoogendorn listened quietly, one big pink hand rubbing her forehead.

"Over and *over*. It just never *stops*—" Even Til was surprised to hear the panic in her voice.

"The . . . Ferris wheel?"

Til nodded. What am I *talking* about? she wondered desperately. I just got mixed up on a square root problem and now here I am in the nurse's room talking about Ferris wheels. They'll think I'm nutty—

"When did you last ride on the Ferris wheel, Clotilde?" asked the nurse.

"This morning. No!—No!—Of course not! No—it was yesterday. No—that's not—right—either. It was—Saturday. Yes—*Saturday*—" They're going to lock me up and throw away the key, she told herself. Jeez—telling them I went for a ride on the Ferris wheel on *Monday morning*. What's the *matter* with me?

"Ah. Saturday. You went to Playland on Saturday?"

Til nodded. Better keep my mouth shut, she thought. Things aren't coming out right.

"With your friends? Your parents?"

"Pop. With my—pop." It came out so fast it sounded like Pop! Pop!

"Ah. Clotilde"—the nurse bent over and captured one of Til's flying hands—"tell me, dear, do you—well, do you get along with your father?"

Til blinked again. She wished she could pull the imprisoned hand loose but it really didn't feel all that bad to make a fuss over. "Oh . . . Pop?" she said vaguely. "Sure, we get along . . . swell. He plays the violin."

"The violin. He is a musician?"

" 'Traümerei.' "

"A lovely song." The nurse nodded, waiting for Til to go on.

"By the rocks."

"Clotilde." The nurse pulled a chair close and sat down near Til, still holding her hand, smoothing her fingers over

53

Til's rough knuckles. "Is there—something—you would like to—talk over with—someone?"

Til stared up at her. She was vibrating like a snapped screen-door spring. "I don't—understand—"

"Dear, sometimes . . . sometimes people—children—have, well, *problems*—in their families. And they need to tell someone about it. One shouldn't keep a problem to herself, you know. There may be a way to work it out—"

Til had decided now to get her hand free and was twisting it. The nurse held on tightly.

"Is there . . . something, perhaps, about . . . your father . . . you'd like to tell us?"

Pop? Til shook her head, puzzled. "Pop's all—right—" she said at last. But now all at once she relaxed. At the mention of Pop's name, as warm and loved and comfortable as a favorite blanket, the vibrating springs stopped twanging and her hand lay still, warm as a kitten in the nurse's grasp. The nurse and Mrs. Hoogendorn exchanged a long, quiet look.

"Do you feel better now, Clotilde?" asked the nurse.

"Yes. I do." Til took a long breath.

"You see—it's better to talk things over, isn't it? Aren't you glad you told us?" asked the nurse gently.

"Yes." Til leaned back, and stretched and sighed again. She nodded. "Yes. I'm glad . . . I told you about—the Ferris wheel—"

7

Wednesday turned warmer and Til wore her gray tweed skirt, white blouse, and a blue sweater to school. Since it was nearly the end of the school year, Mrs. Hoogendorn had told them to begin cleaning out their desks. And when Til got off the bus in the afternoon at the bottom of the Quesada Avenue hill, she had her arithmetic and history books to study for finals, a rubber-banded roll of old quiz papers, and her lunch box.

As she walked up the hill and then crossed through the brushy strip, she was aware of a feeling of flattening out, as if all day she had been on a high plain where the sun shone, and now she was descending into a shadowy ravine.

She would have liked to ask Beverly to come over for a while after school, but for a long, long time now, Gertrude had forbidden her to have any friends over. All that dirt, her mother complained, all that mess and extra work. Once in a while now, she could sneak over to Beverly's house on the way home from school, on days when she knew Gertrude would be getting home late; but Til knew that she couldn't go too often. When you couldn't invite somebody over, there was a sharp limit to the number of times you could go to their house, and Beverly was the kind of person who counted things like that. Anyway, Til couldn't decide whether or not she really liked to go there—in a way it only made things worse when she went home. . . .

As she let herself in at the front door, Til thought the house seemed unusually quiet. She stood still for a moment, listening, and then turned toward the stairs. Her room was at the top floor in the back, behind her mother's room. As she mounted the stairs she listened for any sound that would tell her if Gertrude were at home yet, and if so, what she was doing. If possible, Til liked to know where Gertrude was before Gertrude knew where *she* was.

At the top of the stairs she paused and looked back. If Gertrude were in the kitchen, she was being unusually quiet; Gertrude hated to cook, and when she got dinner she always managed to slam things around a lot. The pots and pans and the refrigerator and stove sounded angry and abused, like people in a prisoner-of-war camp being manhandled by the guards. Til had just decided that Gertrude had not come home yet—perhaps was working late—when the slightest sound behind her made her jerk around.

As usual she was not quick enough. A stinging blow cracked across the side of her face. She lost her balance and felt herself lifted and thrown outward into the space of the stairwell, and then she was clattering and rolling over and over down the stairs. Her tin lunch box bumped down after her, splitting open and scattering pieces of waxed paper, crusts of bread, and cookie crumbs. As she landed at the foot of the stairs, her Thermos bottle hit the floor beside her and she could hear the sodden crash of splintered glass inside it.

There was a moment of absolute silence, and then a shriek from above her. Gertrude came pounding down the stairs, awkward and heavy, her face convulsed with rage. "Your Thermos!" she screamed. "YOU BROKE YOUR THER-MOS BOTTLE!"

Til stared up at her, dazed.

Gertrude reached the foot of the stairs and leaned over, seized Til by the shoulder and dragged her up. She held her half dangling, off-balance, while she shouted in her face: "It isn't bad enough to lie and sneak—no!—you have to break things—ruin things—smash things, too!" Her hot, bad-smelling breath smothered Til, and Til tried to turn her face. Gertrude yanked her around again.

"I—don't—understand—" gasped Til. She was still stunned from the fall but had barely begun to hurt yet. "*I* didn't—drop it—you pushed—"

"You don't understand? No, you *never* understand, do you? No—you lie and sneak and—and—do every bad thing you can think of—and then you come in here—into *my* house—all innocent—pretend you don't know anything at all—cover up! But I'm not fooled—you've let it slip, now—"

"Let *what* slip?" Til whispered desperately. Her face was beginning to swell and her lips felt funny. They didn't make the words right.

"Don't play innocent with me! You think just because I—you think I'm your slave, don't you? You think you can sneak off—with—with—and then come back here—to *my* house—and laugh—*laugh!* about me—"

"I'm—not—laughing—"

"All of you—you're laughing—you think I'm just your

slave—work—all day. Clean house—all night. Nobody cares about me—care about other people—not me! I just earn—paycheck—support *you*—you think—I'm just your *slave*!''

Gertrude was getting back to familiar ground. Till wondered desperately if the end of this explosion was in sight. She tried to stand absolutely still, keep her mouth shut.

"Laughing—" Gertrude's eyes glittered and she was smiling now. Til could not understand why her mother smiled, or what she had in her other hand, passing it back and forth in front of Til's eyes.

Til squinted, tried to catch the figures on the paper. It was a picture—a photograph. Two figures—a girl and a big man—yes! The photograph was her and Pop—taken on Market Street last Saturday by the street photographer.

"That's my picture," she mumbled, forgetting her resolve not to say anything more. "Where—did you—get it?"

"*Your* picture? Who said it was *your* picture!" cried Gertrude. "I say it's *my* picture. Everything in this house is *mine*—" Gertrude drew herself up like a crazy queen, staring wildly around the shabby house. "Everything here is mine! *I* work to pay the bills. Do *you* work—?" Til shook her head slowly. "*I* scrub and clean everything. Do *you* scrub?" Til shook her head again. She felt as if she were being hypnotized as her head went back and forth. "So!" shouted Gertrude triumphantly, "then it's *mine*!"

Til's head ached. She found herself wondering dimly if perhaps that might not be true. It was a fact that Gertrude did work to pay the bills—Pop's contributions were not large and occasionally he seemed to forget about them altogether for a month or so. Maybe since Gertrude did support the home—and also took care of it—maybe it *was* hers, to do whatever

58

she wanted with it and to it, and to anyone who lived in it—

But not the picture. "That's mine," Til said more clearly now. "Pop paid for it and it's mine." She reached out a hand to try to grab it.

"Oh—ho!" Gertrude suddenly released her and danced back, still holding the picture. "Now I see it all! He takes *you* out for the day—nobody ever takes *me* anyplace! And then you both sneak off to her and he buys you a picture"— she waved it tantalizingly just out of Til's reach—"from *her!*"

Til blinked. She was getting very tired of stumbling after Gertrude trying to get hold of the picture. Gertrude would race up the stairs a few steps, then down a few steps, dodging back and forth, holding the picture just out of reach, as if she were playing a game. Til could only see blurry glimpses of the photograph. It was like keep-away at school, where somebody grabbed your book or scarf or pen and then you had to jump and dodge and scramble to try to get it back.

Suddenly Gertrude slipped past her and raced down the stairs. As she ran across the hall, through the living room and into the kitchen, Til heard her laughing. "Mine! It's mine now—*mine!*"

Til sank slowly down onto the stairs. She was trembling and exhausted. Her mind was in a jumble, as if it were a bucket of odds and ends that had rolled down the stairs, mixing everything up. "I'll sort it all out," she said idiotically, "in just a minute. In just a minute—in just a minute—"

8

She sat on the stairs for a long time, as the afternoon grew old and turned into evening. Most of the time she just looked at the scattered papers and garbage at the foot of the stairs, the smashed Thermos with a puddle of milk leaking out. For some reason she could not explain she no longer wanted to go up to her room. For one thing, it was at the back of the house—at the end of the hall—a *dead* end—

As the light grew dimmer and dimmer, her head cleared. The scene at the school, in the nurse's room, returned to her, and she decided to think about that. Carefully, to occupy herself, she went over every detail, but finally could only feel puzzled about it. "The Ferris wheel," she said at last. "I wonder why I told them about the Ferris wheel. . . ."

At last she got up. She gathered up the mess at the foot of the stairs and carried it on tiptoe to the bathroom. She placed the food scraps and pieces of waxed paper in the wastepaper basket, got an old washcloth and wet it, and went back and rubbed up the spots on the floor.

There was a light in the kitchen, some noises, and Gertrude appeared to be cooking dinner.

Til's stomach lurched. She was aching and very tired, and would have been hungry, she supposed, if her head didn't ache so bad. She was trying hard to think—it was like the problem in square roots: You should think of what seemed to be a *reasonable* answer. But what was the reasonable answer here? If she went up to her room, Gertrude would come storming up there after her, and Til recognized panic in her own unwillingness to be in that little room with Gertrude between her and the door. Or she could go out into the kitchen and sit down at the table and try to eat. Or she could just turn around and go out the door and down the street—

But where could she go?

The neighbors were all strangers to her—odds and ends of people who had lately moved into the houses on the block. These days people moved abruptly about the country: some to be near a relative on an army base or naval installation, others to fit themselves into the vast surging mass of people who were engaged in "war work"—jobs in shipyards, airplane factories, munitions plants. People were intensely and painfully preoccupied with concerns and grief and troubles of their own; none of them was likely to be interested in Til; still less, helpful.

Pop would welcome her, she was sure, but his tiny apartment was clear over in Pacific Heights, two long bus rides away. And even with Gertrude on the rampage, Til couldn't quite bring herself to attempt it. Especially when the only thing Pop could do was to bring her right back. Gertrude, he had made absolutely clear to Til from the first, had been awarded custody of her daughter by the court during the divorce proceedings. It was an automatic decision—a mother was always given custody of her children, and there had not been the slightest discussion about it, or any chance at all for Til to speak on her own behalf.

No one had asked Til which parent she would have preferred to live with; when they all left the courtoom that day, it was like being on a desert island and watching the only rescue boat pull away from the shore without her as Pop walked down the corridor alone, leaving her standing there with Gertrude. Of course he had promised Til that he would come for her every Saturday, and he had kept his promise. But Saturday was only one day out of the week, and that left six other days to get through. She knew from quiet, discreet questioning that such custody settlements were almost never changed; the future, as far as she could see, was set in cement.

That left exactly no place to go, no place to run to. She thought longingly of the school nurse and of Mrs. Hoogendorn, the teacher, but of course she had no idea where either of them lived. There was no telephone in the house—Gertrude would not allow one—but even if she could get to a phone, find them in the San Francisco telephone book (a job for Ellery Queen)—then what could she say to them?—"My mother and I had a fight and I felt lonesome—please talk to me?" They probably think I'm batty already, after the way I talked about the Ferris wheel on Monday. Just imagine what they'd think if I called one of them up at this time of day and told them my mother hit me. I'd find myself locked up at the funny farm for good. . . .

So there was nothing really, then, but the kitchen. And dinner. . . .

Beans and frankfurters and slices of lettuce with mayonnaise. Til sat down on the cold hard kitchen chair and stared

62

silently at the plate in front of her. As usual, after one of her explosions, Gertrude had become very quiet, with a curious air of having triumphed over some adversary. Strangely enough her manner seemed to invite Til to congratulate her, smile upon her and with her, as if Gertrude had moved another step toward the accomplishment of some goal which was still hidden in the mists of the future, but was beginning to loom larger and larger, like the shadow of someone against a window curtain at night.

Til sensed the presence of the goal, the way she might look far down a road she was traveling and see a speck of some kind. She worried a little about what the speck might be when she got to it, but most of the time she was so occupied with the things that were happening right here, right now, that she did not have time to worry about the speck. And after one of her explosions, Gertrude always seemed to be in an unusually good humor—sometimes even faintly friendly. It was during these times that Til was most comfortable and at peace, oddly enough, and then she could not bring herself to spoil the brief moment of respite by worrying about the speck. . . .

The only sounds in the kitchen were the clicking of forks and knives on plates, the hiss of a gas burner under the teakettle, the wind rattling the windowpanes. The tall old-fashioned windows were misty with steam, and the air felt clammy and damp. As usual there was no heat on and Til felt chilled. She shivered, and then sneezed.

"Are you catching a cold?" asked Gertrude sharply, staring at her from across the table.

Til shook her head.

"Speak up. I can't hear you."

"No . . . no. No—cold. My throat—sore—" Til croaked. Her throat was sore, now that she thought about it. She ached all over too, but then, what else—?

"You'd better go to bed." Gertrude rose and started to clear the table. "Go to bed. I'll do the dishes."

Til cringed, waiting for it to start all over again. Normally it was her responsibility to do the dinner dishes, and if she didn't get them done—

She made a movement as if to walk to the sink, but Gertrude directed her out of the room with a jerk of her head. "Go to bed," said Gertrude.

Til sighed and then turned away. She dragged herself across the kitchen, but as she was passing the corner of the counter nearest the door, her eye was caught. The picture—the photograph—of herself and Pop was carefully propped against the sugar cannister. She saw now that something had been written across the bottom of the picture in ink—*To Til—best wishes and a million laughs—from Pop and Helga.* Thoughts flashed hazily through Til's head: the jolly blonde photographer—Pop standing there blinking and smiling—*Helga?*—So *that* was why Sigmund-the-Figmund stopped! He *knew* Helga—

But now Til saw something else. There was a space down the middle of the picture. It had been cut in half and then the two sections propped up close together with a gap in between. Til shivered suddenly, but she barely paused and she said nothing, only walked on. She climbed the stairs after a short pause at the bathroom and went on to her bedroom. Finally there, and with the door shut behind her, she let out a long, tightly held breath. After a few moments she undressed and crawled under the covers, although it was much earlier than she usually went to bed. She fell asleep abruptly, as if she had been hit on the head.

Sometime during the night she awoke. At first she supposed that it was only the throbbing ache in her head, her sore ribs, the bruised knee, that roused her. Then she realized that someone—Gertrude—was in the room. At once she was alarmed, although she made no sound at all to show she was awake.

She watched Gertrude through slit eyes. The hall light was on as usual, and she could see that her mother was still dressed, although it was long past the time when Gertrude normally went to bed. She even had the knitting needles still thrust through the knot in her hair.

Gertrude seemed to be drifting aimlessly around the room, touching things—the dresser, the curtains, the chair, the closet door, a picture, a lamp. She was whispering something to herself, but Til could not hear it. Once she picked up a belt of Til's from the chest and tried to fasten it around her own waist, but of course it was several inches too short. Then she came to stand by the bed, still carrying the belt, and stared down at Til.

Til could feel sweat breaking out on her even in the cold room. How long could she force herself to remain absolutely still?

After what seemed like a century, Gertrude turned abruptly and walked out of the room, still carrying the belt.

Til crept silently out of bed and put on her robe. She

pulled some heavy socks on her feet and took an extra blanket from the closet. Then she crept soundlessly down the stairs into the bathroom, locked the door, and, wrapping up in the blanket, lay down on the floor and slept. . . .

9

A problem in square roots. As the bus roared down Third Street, belching stinking blue smoke, Til sat slumped in her seat, her tin lunch pail and books on her lap, staring out the window at the early morning traffic, the patchy fog.

She always used this time on the bus in the morning to work out her problems, do her thinking. Whatever subject was up for consideration on that day was sorted over, examined, dissected and disposed of during the bus ride to school. Sometimes she did a little research: sex, the equinoxes, why some people have curly hair and some don't. How can I get another pair of shoes now that I've used all my shoe ration stamps? Most of the time she could work things out; occasionally the mere passage of time brought some answers: Kotex is used for something called *the curse*; the curse is something that happens every month to girls; oh, so *this* is the curse!

But it was beginning to be clear to her (no! not just beginning—it had been clear for a long time, but she had refused to acknowledge it) that the present problem with Gertrude was not one she could solve by herself. And that, of course, was what made it so hard. For as long as she could remember, she had always felt that she had no one to rely on but herself—Pop didn't (or couldn't) understand, and Gertrude—Gertrude was . . . well, what *was* Gertrude? Other kids could go to their mothers when they had a problem, were frightened about something. But where did you go . . . when your mother *was* the problem?

It wasn't as if it had always been this way. Although she could not remember a time when they had been a really happy family, at least there were times—way back—when it hadn't been so bad. No, the really bad times had started shortly after Pop left the house. Pop, she realized, had left because he thought his going would calm Gertrude and make her less irritable, easier to get along with. Instead, his absence seemed to Til only to provoke her mother to still greater extremes, as if she now had time and opportunity to focus *all* her anger on Til, instead of just part of it.

What her mother was angry about, Til could not puzzle out. Over and over her mother screamed that she—Til—was dirty, destructive, insolent, uncontrollable. The least infraction of a minor rule was enough to provoke severe punishment. At first Til had really tried to avoid making mistakes, but then Gertrude just invented mistakes Til had never heard of. It was wrong to cough or sneeze, wrinkle your skirt, whistle, run more than an inch of water in the tub for a bath, disarrange a curtain or a pillow, leave a crumb of food on your plate, ask for a second helping—or, in fact, ask for anything. Mistakes were everywhere and punishment so constant that finally Til came to see her life as simply a progression from one mistake to another, and found herself continuously on edge, waiting for the next one to occur. It was like wading

68

in muddy water that concealed sharp rocks on which you were bound to stub your toe, but for some reason you couldn't get out of the water onto dry land.

As time went by, she began to accumulate an unusual concentration of bruises, welts, blisters, swellings. She thought Pop might see and ask where they came from, but he seemed too busy to notice them, or else he thought they were the normal wear and tear of an active girl. Both Mrs. Hoogendorn and the school nurse had taken notice of them, though, and immediately began to ask quiet, casual questions. But for some reason, obscure even to herself, she could never force herself to tell anyone the truth about how she got them. It had something to do with shame, but she was not sure whether the shame was Gertrude's . . . or Pop's . . . or hers. . . .

Other kids didn't have marks on them.

Other kids' skin was clear and unblemished; hers was blotched with red marks slowly turning dirty-looking and black. Scabs peeled. Cuts bled. Joints stiffened and hurt. Her head ached because under the cover of her hair there were lumps that never went down, sticky scabs where cuts in the scalp bled. If her head would just stop hurting, she thought she could probably figure out the problem—in square roots, of course—

She got off the bus with the others and then turned aside at the playground gate. Forfeiting those last delicious minutes of uproar with the other kids before the bell would ring, she turned and walked, alone, all the way around the schoolyard. She felt queer and a little giddy. The day was clear and warm—for San Francisco—and beyond the iron edge of the city and The Embarcadero with its piers thrusting out like naked ribs, she could see whitecaps frothing up in the blue water of the bay. Above it all, great misty clumps of fog, broken loose from the offshore bank, were drifting inland where they would soon evaporate above the Livermore hills and the dry San Joaquin valley. It was a beautiful day. A kind, warm, and beautiful day. If only her head didn't hurt so much—

She would talk to Mrs. Hoogendorn again. She could not really tell when the idea had solidified, but it might have been when the bus driver had miscalculated and flipped the wheel of the bus over a curb as they rounded a corner. The subsequent jolt made Til's head throb and swim; at that moment she acknowledged through the blur that things couldn't go on this way forever—

She stood behind the wastebasket near Mrs. Hoogendorn's desk, her fingers drumming noisily on the arm of the teacher's chair. Mrs. Hoogendorn was surrounded by hordes of other kids who were full of a million questions. Every time Til opened her mouth to start a remark that she hoped Mrs. Hoogendorn would pick up on, some nut barged up and asked a dumb question like How far away is the sun? What did you call the venous system of the liver? or When was the Magna Carta—whatever that might be—signed?

Til watched the clock. Mrs. Hoogendorn allowed them to cluster around her desk until exactly thirty seconds before nine. Then she would shoo them all back to their own desks to take their books out and be ready to go to work on the stroke of nine.

The second hand on the big wall clock was sweeping its last round by the time Til got an opening.

"Mrs. Hoogendorn—" she gasped. "Can you—help me? I can't—don't know what—please tell me—"

Mrs. Hoogendorn glanced up, but Til could see that her attention was on the clock.

"—Can't figure out—can you help—" It was crazy the way her chest and throat tightened up just now, when she was finally trying to get some help. "—Got to have—help—"

Mrs. Hoogendorn raised her eyebrows briefly. She put out a pink hand to direct Til back to her seat.

"I—have this—problem—" Til searched desperately for a word with which to describe the indescribable, the fear, the pain, the shame. I should have thought of something to call it, she thought hopelessly, before I started to tell her.

Mrs. Hoogendorn nodded. "Yes. I know you're having trouble with square roots, Clotilde. We'll go over it again during third period, and I'm sure we'll be able to get you straightened out. Take your seat, now. It's nine o'clock."

If she moved fast enough she could get to the nurse's room before it closed at the end of the school day. Mrs. Foley, the nurse, was a large, gentle, untidy, slow-moving woman, who was never quite on time. When the final bell rang, ending the last period of the day, there were usually a few minutes left before the nurse's room closed, as Mrs. Foley busied herself clearing her desk, making notes, washing thermometers, and checking her supplies.

Desperately Til lunged against the current (everyone else was going out, she was going in) and the mob nearly rode her down. She dodged and sidestepped, made six steps ahead, lost three, made two more. Everybody was yelling, and the thunder of their feet sounded like a buffalo stampede going down the hall.

At last, wet with sweat, Til found herself in the hall outside the nurse's room. The door was open and the light still on.

She came to a halt, staring at the door. After the intense effort of getting there—after thinking about it all day—she found that she had traveled exactly as far as she could. The door was only two feet away, but she could not cross the threshold. Her heart thudded and she suddenly felt more exhausted than she had ever been in her life. She stood staring down at her feet.

Suddenly a shadow appeared on the floor. She raised her head. Mrs. Foley, her hand on the doorknob, ready to close and lock the door, was standing there looking at her.

There was a long silence, and then the nurse spoke. "Is there something . . . did you want to see me, Clotilde?"

Til nodded dumbly.

The nurse hesitated only a second, and then beckoned her into the room. As the door closed behind her, Til felt total panic. What am I going to do? What am I going to say?

The nurse motioned her into a chair, and Til sat but immediately sprang out of it again. On rubbery legs that threatened to collapse any moment, she began to pace around the room.

The nurse busied herself casually with a box of tongue depressers, counting them. At last she said, "Clotilde, can't you sit down?"

Til shook her head. She was trembling.

"I see. Then *I'll* sit down." Mrs. Foley placed her large backside into her swivel chair and folded her hands on her stomach. Her face was very quiet, very kind.

72

"Can you talk now, Clotilde?"

Til opened her mouth but nothing came out.

The nurse nodded. "Then *I'll* talk." She smiled faintly. "Clotilde—we've been—well, watching you for some time. No," she added quickly, seeing the panic on Til's face, "not in a *bad* way, dear. We know—how shall I put it?—we know that it's not *you* who is doing something wrong. But something wrong *is* being done. By someone. The question is—by whom? And what is it?"

She paused. Til lifted one foot and placed it a few inches closer to the nurse's desk. She was listening intently.

"Now—the other day when you were in here, you told us about . . . a ride on the Ferris wheel." She paused, waited to see if Til would say anything, then went on. "You said that on Saturday your father took you out to Playland and that you rode the Ferris wheel. You said"—she was watching Til's face intently, was rewarded by seeing that Til took one more step toward the desk—"you said that the Ferris wheel made you sick—"

Til was sweating. "Throws me. Up and—down. It keeps throwing me—hits me and throws me—" she whispered.

The nurse nodded, very carefully. "You see, dear, it's very strange about people. Sometimes when we are afraid of a person, we change that person, in our minds of course, into a thing. Like an animal, or maybe . . . a Ferris wheel. Do you understand me, Clotilde?"

Til squinted her eyes and then forced them open. Odd. She'd never thought of *that*—

"So . . . I'm wondering if maybe . . . you aren't afraid of the Ferris wheel—if the Ferris wheel makes you so sick—because it—represents your *father*?"

73

Til stared blankly. All the ground she had gained was suddenly lost.

"We know that your parents are divorced," continued the nurse quietly. "And we know that your father comes to see you on Saturday—that he takes you to ride the Ferris wheel. Clotilde"—suddenly and without warning it came—"Clotilde, is your father beating you?"

A cry of despair came from somewhere deep inside her and escaped through her mouth. Til was astonished by its strength. It was like a wild animal running away from someone who would capture it and hold it in; the sound had to get out—get out—

All the way down the hall, out the door, across the schoolyard, down the street, running, she could still hear the cry, free now, but wasted, because nobody had understood what it tried to say—

She did not see the nurse who lumbered along after her but was left behind when Til sprang through the gaping doors of the Third Street bus.

10

The afternoon sun slanted down almost even with the steep slope of Quesada Avenue as Til walked up the hill from the bus stop, crossing through the center strip of shrubbery. Her tin lunch box (lighter now since there was no Thermos in it) banged against her thigh. She had no books since the school term was nearly at an end and finals were over now; all she carried were a few odds and ends of pencils and an old notebook from history class.

She had gone by Beverly's house to put off going home, but Beverly's older brother had answered the door. "Sick," he said curtly to Til's inquiring look. "Mother said for her to stay in bed and not have any company. So you'll have to go on home." His arms were full of textbooks; Til knew he was planning to enlist in the air corps next month, and he was totally indifferent to any problem of hers. He closed the door before she had a chance to say good-bye. Even then she had sat on the front steps for a while to put off leaving. She pretended to tie her shoes—both of them—because she knew that Hank, Beverly's brother, might glance out through the dining room window; but even that feeble excuse ran out at last. It was very hard, going back down the walk of Beverly's house without having been allowed to pass a little time in there where things appeared to be so different from her own home. But Hank would be watching, making sure she didn't double back and sneak in to waste any more of his valuable time. . . .

Til squinted up the hill, trying to tell from the way the house looked whether or not Gertrude was home. Normally her mother's shift at the plant ran from eight in the morning until five in the afternoon, and then it took her at least forty-five minutes to reach home on the bus. But lately there had been times when Gertrude reached the house ahead of Til—probably by taking sick leave and getting off work early. The memory of yesterday's attack was scaldingly fresh; if Gertrude was home, Til had no intention of letting her mother come up behind her again.

So I've got to . . . watch, she told herself. Keep my eyes open.

Immediately she felt her head start to ache. It always happened this way. Whenever she tried to force herself to confront her situation—to really face up to it—her head started to ache and her heart pound. Her stomach would either hurt or turn nauseous, and finally she would be in such physical misery that she would simply drop the whole thing like a heavy load. At such times she usually went to bed and slept for a while—using the excuse of a sick headache—until, with the passage of an hour or so (and putting her mother completely out of her mind) she felt better.

Actually, it was only by means of *not* thinking about things that she was holding on. Occasionally short glimpses (like scenes through a crack of a partly open door) slipped through her defenses: Gertrude dragging out a mop and bucket of soapsuds to clean up a couple of cracker crumbs on the floor, Gertrude walking around talking to herself, the way her answers didn't always match up with what you had said to her, and always, always, the explosions.

For a long time Til had kidded herself about them. At first she bragged, like the other kids did, about how harsh her mother was. Everybody bellyached about their folks— whatever punishment your girl friend got for breaking dishes or sassing somebody, you tried to top it with your own horror story. You took great pride in being tough. But Til quickly found that the other kids thought she was lying. Nobody believed that Gertrude knocked her down for dropping the dish towel on the floor. Nobody believed that Gertrude came up behind her and pushed her face down into the water (almost too long) when she forgot to turn the tap off and ran more water than she needed in the bathtub.

And of course Til did not believe it either. She knew there had to be a sensible explanation for her mother's actions. Even though they complained, all the other kids agreed, at bottom, that your mother loved you—really—and did everything she could to take care of you and provide what was best for you. *Therefore* (like in the problem of square roots), if one answer didn't seem to make sense, then you had to go further and find a better one. If your mother was *right,* then you must be *wrong.*

So for a long time that had been the answer to the problem. She's right and I'm wrong. I'm sloppy and lazy and dirty and insolent. I must be. My mother says so and everybody knows that your mother is always right. Jean Simmons's mother is right. Elizabeth McLean's nother is right. Victoria Johnson's mother is right. So—*my* mother must be right too.

It was the best answer she could find and for a long time it worked. Gertrude had told her that she was "out of control" now that Pop had moved out of the house, and that although she—Til—thought she could do anything she wanted, Gertrude would continue the struggle to teach her better behavior. In a way it made sense. Til knew for a fact that she occasionally did things like break a glass or throw something nowadays that she didn't do before Pop left. But were the things she did as bad as Gertrude said they were? They must be, because if your mother said something then it was right. . . .

That really was the trouble with it all, she thought as she stood looking up at the house. My head's aching—I can hardly think. I don't *know* what's right and what's wrong. She's cranky, but maybe no more so than anyone else. If I just had some way to tell—if something would show me—*I've got to be sure*—"

She let herself in the front door and stood still, listening. The house was quiet, but then it always was. She set her lunch box, notebook and pencils down without a sound (behind the umbrella stand, for some reason) and then turned toward the stairs. She would see if Gertrude were upstairs before she went through the house to the kitchen.

From long practice she had found out how to get up and down the stairs without making a sound. Moving like a shadow, she searched the two bedrooms and hall; no one there. If Gertrude were home, she wasn't up here. Til picked up her winter coat, which was lying on the floor in her room (did *I* leave it there?), and absentmindedly carried it with her as she descended the stairs again.

On the first floor again she stopped to listen. She thought she heard a noise but couldn't be sure. The living room was empty and so was the bathroom.

But when she stood in the kitchen door, even though Gertrude was not there, Til could see that her mother had been home, had been here in the kitchen. There was a pan on the stove, steaming a little. A couple of empty vegetable cans were in the sink, and the table was set for dinner.

For *dinner?*

Til's skin crawled as she stared at the table. At her own place was a plate, a glass, a silver fork, knife, and spoon.

At her mother's place was neither plate nor cup. Just a row of butcher knives. . . .

11

Til pulled on her coat and, thinking rather clearly considering the kitchen table, she reached up and grabbed the broken cup that held the money Gertrude always left to pay the paper boy and the milkman. There were at least three or four dollars in the cup—and even as her hand closed over the money, she knew that Gertrude would kill her for taking it. I'm in a corner, she thought desperately. If I take the money she'll kill me. If I *don't*—?

She looked for one more second at the knives on the table. Well, I wanted a sign. I wanted something to tell me if she is really—

The thing is: What is a butcher knife for?

To cut with.

And what is there to cut with a butcher knife when all you're having to eat is beans and potatoes—?

Til turned and ran quietly back to the front hall. She got her lunch box from its hiding place, picked up the pencils and notebook so Gertrude would not immediately guess she had been there (until she discovered the empty cup), and let herself out the door.

She was halfway down the hill again, running hard, before it occurred to her: my head doesn't ache anymore—

"Could I please use your telephone?" inquired Gertrude politely of Mrs. Fundy at the house next door. Old Mrs. Fundy was hard of hearing and you had to shout at her, but she did have a phone, and once in a while when the need was urgent, Gertrude asked to borrow it.

Mrs. Fundy stared blankly at her, and Gertrude raised her hands to pantomime a phone call. Mrs. Fundy nodded and beckoned her into the house.

Gertrude tiptoed carefully over to the little walnut table by the lace-curtained window where the phone sat. Her apron pockets sagged heavily with the load of butcher knives, and the handles poked her in the leg, but she had not wanted to leave them behind in the house. After coming up from the basement where she had been dusting the paint cans, she had decided to make a phone call to *him*—Helmut—so she just scooped them up and brought them along. They gave her a nice feeling, clinking away down deep in her pockets. Mrs. Fundy, deaf as a post, could not hear the nice sound, of course, nor a single word anyone said.

Gertrude gave the operator Helmut's number and waited while it rang.

The phone was lifted at the other end, and she heard Helmut's thick German voice. "Yah? Yah?"

"Helmut?"

"Yah?"

"This is Gertrude."

"Yah? Yah? Hello? Well—?" He waited a second for her to speak.

Gertrude frowned. What was it she had wanted to tell him? Her mind was a little confused these days—there had been so much *trouble* lately, with Til.

—Ah, that must be it. She must have planned to tell him all about the trouble. "Til—" she began, "I wanted to tell you about Til—"

"Yah?" said Helmut when she paused. "What about Til?"

"Trouble," said Gertrude with difficulty. Odd how hard it was for her speak all at once. She felt as if there were a cord tied tightly around her throat, trapping all the words down inside her where they might easily explode and hurt someone—maybe even her. "So much—*trouble*—it has to stop now. I must put a stop to it once and for all— The money is gone—Til—*trouble*—"

"What kind of trouble? Gertrude? Are you still there? Answer me—what kind of trouble is Til having? What can I do to help her?"

Oh, my. He had not understood after all. Gertrude sighed and slowly put the phone back on its hook. Here she had come all the way over to Mrs. Fundy's house to call Helmut and explain to him that Til was causing so much trouble that she was going to have to put a stop to it—now—forever—and Helmut thought it was *Til* who needed help.

Mrs. Fundy glanced at Gertrude and Gertrude smiled.

"He didn't understand," she said politely, although she knew, of course, that Mrs. Fundy couldn't hear a word. "He didn't understand that *I'm* the one who needs help. And that I will have to *do something* about Til. I'm going to have to put a stop—to all this trouble—" She fingered a knife in her pocket. "I will just have to do it tonight. I can't possibly put up with any more of her trouble. Why, would you believe it—only the other day she actually *broke her Thermos bottle?* And now this—taking the money. But I will put a stop to it. When she comes home . . .''

With her hand still in her pocket on one of the knives, Gertrude said good-bye and thank you to Mrs. Fundy and went back to her own house.

Helmut Foerester set the phone back on its hook and stood for a while frowning down at it. Odd. Gertrude almost never called him—and then only when he had failed to send her the monthly check for Til's support. They never spoke to each other at all anymore—a source of relief for Helmut, who felt he heard all he wanted to hear about Gertrude from Til. . . .

. . . Or did he, come to think of it? Suddenly a little feeling of uneasiness, unrest, began to creep over him, like a draft of cold air under a door. When was the last time Til had mentioned Gertrude? After a thorough search of his memory, Helmut realized that it had been weeks—months, maybe— since Til had said one single word about Gertrude.

Now that was odd. Til talked like a magpie, as if talking was going out of style and she wanted to enjoy it as much as possible while she could. She talked about school, Mrs. Hoogendorn, Beverly, Beverly's brother, baseball, movies, books, jokes, the war—anything and everything. But not, he suddenly realized, about Gertrude.

Why wouldn't Til mention Gertrude at least once in a while? It didn't seem natural for a child as young as Til not to say from time to time, "Mom said—'' or "Mom did so-and-so—''

Helmut took a coffeepot down off the shelf above the sink,

filled it with water, threw in some coffee, and set it on the single burner electric plate he had to cook with. While the water started to warm, to steam, and finally to bubble up inside the glass dome in the lid, he walked over to the window and stood looking out at the steep slant down Pacific Avenue to Van Ness Avenue.

Shouldn't have left her there alone. Yes, it had been a mistake to leave Til alone with Gertrude. Especially since Gertrude was such a strange, hot-tempered person. Not that she would ever really *hurt* Til—he was sure of that—but . . .

The truth of the matter was he simply couldn't force himself to stay there with Gertrude any longer. Great God in Heaven—there had to be something better in life than screaming and fighting all the time. He had tried for a long while to get along with her, but at last had realized that it simply couldn't be done. With Gertrude it was always a battle, a war; and Helmut was a man utterly unfit for anything but peace. Just to sit and chat, maybe have a few beers, tell some jokes. . . . What else did life have to offer, after all? And if he gave up the struggle, left the house, wasn't it going to be better in the long run for Til to have a sane father who still had a paycheck coming in, rather than maybe a father who drank all the time because he was so unhappy—possibly even to the point of losing his job? Surely Til was safer with him out of the house, away from Gertrude, than with him there and fighting with her day and night.

When the coffee was perked, Helmut drank a cup and ate a bologna sandwich. Time to go to work, he saw. When you were a stevedore, you worked odd hours.

Before he left the apartment, he wrote a note: *Helga—Gertrude called. Something about Til and trouble—* He repeated

84

it in German to make sure she understood. *I don't know what to do. Maybe I have to go over there tomorrow. In pot is coffee. I love you. Gut nacht.*

He smiled a little as he folded the note and put it beside the coffeepot. Such a thing for a fat old German fiddle-player to say: I love you. But he did. He did love Helga. Helga, the crazy blonde street photographer whom he met because she always ate her meals at the same neighborhood cafe where he had his. Helga . . .

Maybe there was something good in life after all, he thought as he pulled on his boots. Lately he had begun to hope—really hope—again. Helga was so good, so sane. After all, with the divorce final now, Helmut was free to marry again. Then there would be a home—a *real* home—not this terrible coffin of a room, stinking and dirty and lonely, and he could at least bring Til to that home on their Saturdays instead of always having to take her out to Playland. God in Heaven, how tired he was of Playland—the noise, the people, the popcorn, the rides. No—with Helga now there was something to look forward to—things were going to get better.

Helmut touched the paper again with one big stubby finger. Helga would see the note. Helga would understand. The first good thing to happen in a long time had been his meeting Helga . . . and at last he could begin to see some daylight at the far end of the tunnel—

At the bottom of the Quesada Avenue hill, Til slowed to a jog and then came to a halt.

The thing was—where could she go? She knew she had some distant cousins—relatives of Gertrude's and therefore suspect—who lived in San Diego. Pop's family, of course, was still in Germany; there were no friendly aunts and uncles, no fat, comfortable grandmothers in Til's life to whom she could turn for comfort and advice.

Other possibilities? She had heard of people begging sanctuary in a church, and that Gothic idea translated into the language of the year 1943 would mean having a talk with your priest or minister. But what if you didn't have a church? There were several churches not too far away, and probably hundreds throughout San Francisco, of every known denomination and cult, but Til had never so much as set foot in a church in her life. Gertrude hated churches and swore they were only after your money. Til, being a stranger to churches, was uncertain as to whether any of them would take her in, much less listen to her, or help. . . .

Mrs. Hoogendorn? Leaning (around the corner on Third Street, out of sight of the house) against the rough brick wall of a building, Til thought longingly of her teacher. Mrs. Hoogendorn was in charge of reasonable answers. But Mrs. Hoogendorn was a Monday-through-Friday-in-the-classroom person, not to mention the fact that Til had already demonstrated to herself that when she tried to talk to Mrs. Hoogendorn, things just didn't come out right. If anything, they got worse. . . .

For a moment, as she leaned back, eyes closed, Til allowed herself time to curse her own stupidity. Why didn't I try harder to tell Mrs. Hoogendorn or Mrs. Foley? Why did I act so dumb, so silly? They would have helped me . . . I think. Anyway, they *tried* to help me. Even though they didn't really understand—they knew something was wrong and they were trying to help.

86

But they had it figured out wrong, and that's why I couldn't talk to them, make them understand. They thought it was Pop. I kept getting things all mixed up: Saturday, Pop, the Ferris wheel. It's no wonder they didn't understand—

Slowly Til's knees folded and she sank down on the sidewalk, hugging her legs for warmth. The wind had come up and she was very cold. She stared at the small, shabby business houses on either side of Third Street, most of them closed now, after six o'clock. North of Hunters Point was the long row of piers where the ships lay to, loading and unloading around the clock like furious machines that gobbled up or disgorged freight. Several cars, a bus or two, and a few pedestrians went by. No one glanced at her, or even seemed to know she was there, sitting with her back against the cooling bricks. She had never felt so alone in her life, and slowly (like an optical illusion) the picture began to shift.

Really, it must be *my* fault, she told herself at last. I'm dumb. *I'm* the one who's crazy. I must be. I never heard of anyone else who thinks the things I do. I must be the crazy one. Why else would I start talking about a Ferris wheel on Monday morning. *It must be me—*

Then all at once the street changed. Where before the house had seemed dangerous and threatening and the street safe, now suddenly the street was dangerous and the house seemed safe.

I'm crazy. That's it—*I'm* crazy. I just don't understand. There was probably a good reason why Mom had all those knives on the table. Your *mother* wouldn't put butcher knives on the table without a good, sane reason. I just didn't understand.

The evening air was cool and crisp as she climbed the hill

again. She felt light and strong, free, easy, and comfortable. I was wrong. Silly, it's all right. Mom wouldn't do anything to hurt—

Walking close to the houses, partly concealed by flights of steps, garage doors left open, potted trees, she was only fifty feet from the house when she saw Gertrude.

Gertrude did not see her. Til's mother was standing at the foot of the steps, looking up and down the street. "Til? Come here, Til. It's time—I am going to put a stop to all the trouble you are causing now. Til? Til?" She spoke softly, as if she didn't want the neighbors to hear her. And in her hand was the largest butcher knife.

12

Til hid behind the steps of the house down the block for a long time. Gertrude must have stayed out there for an hour or so, walking down a few steps and then up a few steps, talking softly to herself, fingering the knife. Whenever a car went by, or someone on foot, she hid the knife under her sweater. As soon as they were gone, she brought it out again. "Til? It's time. I can't allow you to go on making all this trouble. It has to stop. Til?" she kept saying over and over, as she ran her finger along the blade.

For a long time Til was just afraid. I can't let her see me. She pressed back behind the porch steps, even though she knew Gertrude was not likely to come this far away from her house. As a rule Gertrude stayed strictly in her own house, or on her own porch, her own narrow band of sidewalk, and never ventured out at all unless she was on her way to and from work. Til was fairly sure Gertrude would not find her, even this close to the house, but all the same she stayed hidden until—at last—Gertrude went back into the house.

For a few minutes longer she stayed behind the stairs. She tried to think about what would happen to her if she stood up and went into the house. Gertrude surely knew about the money being gone from the cup by now—she never overlooked anything. And with the knife in her hand—*but your mother loves you*—one blow, one push, one slap with the knife in her hand—*but your mother is always right*—accident, a slash, blood—*but your mother, your mother*—

Til rose and started to run. She ran as fast as she could down the hill, keeping to the side of the street on which the house was located, so that if Gertrude was standing at the front windows, she could not see her. At the corner she crossed the street, still running, and kept on running far down Third Street till she was at a bus stop many blocks from Quesada Avenue.

There was only one place to go now, she realized. Even if it meant two bus rides and a long walk up Market Street to Van Ness alone, at night, there was only one place to go.

She had to find Pop.

She knew, of course, exactly where the apartment was. He had taken her there once, at her insistence, a long time ago. He had needed a lot of persuasion, but she had finally made him understand that if she could just see the place, she would have an "anchor" in her mind; she would be able to picture him there when she could not see him.

The place wasn't a real apartment in a real apartment building, just a single room in an old house that had been cut into several one-room rentals so the landlord could make money off the people who, during wartime, were flooding the city and renting anything and everything that could be found. Til knew Pop was ashamed of the rickety old building, the dirty stairway, the grimy room with its sagging bed, shabby chair, chest and table, the gray washbasin in the corner. Understanding, she had never asked to go there again.

But now, with Gertrude and her knives behind her, Til realized that the worst thing about Pop's apartment was its location. Although he worked as a stevedore on the docks beyond Third Street, his apartment was in Pacific Heights. And that meant that he—and tonight Til—had to ride two buses to cover the distance.

Til wasn't too worried about the Third Street bus. Although she had never ridden it alone at night, she was still familiar with all the buses and drivers on the run. She knew the dirty floors strewn with cigarette butts, the frayed seats, the cracks in the windows of one bus where the wind whistled through. Nobody ever sat by those windows until all the other seats were taken.

She even knew the drivers pretty well on this run: all elderly men who at other times would have been retired and sitting on their front porches watching the world go by. A couple of them had grandchildren in Til's school; one of them, a quiet, soft-spoken Filipino, was a friend of Pop's. She hoped he would be on duty tonight.

Til stood at the bus stop and stared up Third Street. Traffic was light and there were minutes between cars. She had run nearly all the way down the hill to where Third Street crossed the Islais Creek Channel, and the wind whistled among the old warehouses up and down the railroad tracks. The sun was low in the west and soon would be dropping behind the crests of the Twin Peaks. But the shipyards and docks along the bay, of course, were alive with workers and heavy equipment that kept up a steady din. Even so, there were now not many pedestrians on the street. She would, she thought, have to

91

watch out for any police patrols out cruising around; they would lose no time in rounding up a runaway girl and turning her over to her mother.

Til shivered. A stray dog came loping down the street, crossed in front of her, paused to stare at her. His fur was ragged, his eyes gleamed like green lights. He looked wild and hungry and lost . . . like me, she thought dully. If it wasn't for the knives, I'd go home—

From far up the Third Street hill, she now began to hear the peculiar hissing roar of a city bus. Yes, there were the big headlights, the square black bulk, the row of dimly lit windows. In a few seconds the bus slid to a stop in front of her and the folding doors opened.

Til squinted up at the driver. Yes, it was Pop's Filipino friend, Mr. Aguinaldo. Mr. Aguinaldo stared back at her sharply, but said nothing as Til climbed in and put her dime into the hopper. There were only a few passengers on the bus at this hour—silent, tired people coming home from work or going to it. But even with so many seats to choose from, Til picked one right behind the driver.

She sat in silence, staring at the collar of his uniform jacket. It was too big for him—he was a small man, like most Filipinos—and she noticed that he also sat on a cushion so as to raise himself to a better height for driving.

Sometimes when they rode this bus on Saturdays, Pop and Mr. Aguinaldo talked about cockfighting. Pop had never seen a cockfight, wouldn't have gone to see a cockfight if somebody paid him overtime wages, but he was friendly and liked to talk. Mr. Aguinaldo, finding someone congenial to talk with, to lighten the tedium of the long hours, became Pop's friend. And Pop, no matter how crowded Mr. Aguinaldo's bus was, was never left standing on the corner—there was always room for him. Mr. Aguinaldo did not, of course, like Til as well as he liked Pop—she was only a *girl,* after all (he had already told Pop how sorry he was that Pop had no sons)—but even so he kept an eye out for her too. If any of the city's strange people came too close to her or threatened her, Mr. Aguinaldo fixed them with his olive brown eyes, and soon Til would find herself surrounded by a safe, comfortable space.

Til sat in silence, staring out through the smudged, greasy window beside her. She barely noticed the tired shuffle of people boarding and leaving the bus, the creak and groan of the bus itself. Behind her lay Quesada Avenue and the table set for murder; ahead lay Market Street, where she would have to leave this bus and Mr. Aguinaldo's quiet eyes. In between—now—was a quiet place of swaying seat, dull throb of the engine through the bus, and a little time. . . .

The Market Street stop came before she was ready, and Til found herself shuffling toward the door. Just before she climbed down the steps, she turned suddenly toward Mr. Aguinaldo, sitting in the driver's seat. She put out a hand, opened her mouth as if to speak. Then she choked. It was like trying to tell Pop the answer to the Saturday question. So she turned. Descended the steps of the bus. Walked away.

13

It had been a quiet, almost safe ride on Mr. Aguinaldo's bus, but there was nothing quiet or safe about Market Street at this hour. Although it was not all that late—probably only about eight o'clock by now—Til felt as if it were the middle of the night in downtown Hell. She had always loved Market Street, but Market Street in the daytime with crowds of housewives shopping, smart ladies in fur coats and expensive outfits, stores open, and Pop beside her. Now the stores were closed, traffic surged past the sidewalks with gears grinding and ugly impatient horns blowing. The people on the sidewalk were almost all adults now, and it seemed that at least eighty percent of them were sailors. The trim black and white dress uniforms were everywhere.

In the swirling crowd Til stared desperately around for something—someone—familiar. Suddenly the windows of Foster's gleamed just ahead and she plunged through the door.

Abruptly the noise and shuffling crowd and cold wind fell behind her. Warm smells greeted her nose, and the quiet bustle in here was friendly and welcoming. She could almost make herself think she saw Pop's familiar bulky figure in his shabby overcoat and Homburg, sitting at their table by the corner windows.

Til sidled up to the counter, got a tray, and pushed it quickly past the glass cases of food. Her stomach was empty and growling like a lion which had awakened from a nap, and she looked hungrily at the displayed foods. But mindful that her money was short, she took only a sandwich, two frosted doughnuts, and a cup of hot chocolate.

Luckily her favorite little table was empty. Til carried her tray over and seated herself, and immediately grabbed the sandwich and wolfed it down. The bread was dry and the tuna tasteless, but it helped a little to fill up the awful empty place that was opening up just below her rib cage. She crumpled the sandwich wrapper into a ball and put it on her tray, wondering why the sound of paper rattling seemed so loud. It was anything but quiet here in the coffee shop; all around her people were eating and talking, laughing, with coffee cups clinking on saucers, and forks and knives—don't think about knives—

She picked up the hot chocolate and, holding it just under her nose where she could feel the steam coming up in her face, began to sip. It was hot and rich and almost made her feel a little better. For a few seconds she managed to shut everything out and not think at all . . . if only that black shadow over on her right would go away.

Black shadow?

She turned abruptly.

A very large, very drunk sailor was standing so near her

his pea coat was brushing her elbow. She could smell a powerful odor—whiskey?—that was strange and immediately terrifying.

The sailor bent over her. "Hello, there, little lady," he said, and the stench of his peculiar smell washed over her. "How are you tonight?" His voice was thick and mushy, and Til began—like a snail—oozing farther back in her seat. Nothing about her seemed to move but all at once she felt the window pressing against her left shoulder.

"How about—another doughnut, little lady? My treat—" The sailor took a step toward her and he seemed to be hinged in the middle. His legs remained straight but his body was rotating on their base, a few degrees out of plumb as it went around.

Then he folded over in the middle completely and before she knew what was happening he sat down beside her.

Til's head spun. She was locked into the tiny space left her, with the table tight against her chest, the window of the coffee shop on her left, and the vast, sweating, smelly bulk of the drunk sailor pressed against her right side. Then one of his very large hands disappeared, and immediately she felt it fumbling around in her lap.

The hand was like some crazy animal, blind, uncontrollable—hideously dirty and dangerous—

She got her mouth open and tried to push out a scream, or at least curse him, but she had been holding screams in too long and nothing came out.

A black light started to explode in her head when suddenly the dirty animal sprang out of her lap. A second later the vast, stinking bulk of the sailor was peeled away from her side. Shaking and dazed, Til looked up.

96

Two huge sailors with white armbands on their sleeves had seized the drunk and were hauling him off, away from her.

One of them—Til realized dimly now that they were shore patrol—turned to her and started to say something: "Miss—are you alone? Do you need help—?"

But once the way was clear, Til scrambled free of the table and was out the door and down the sidewalk, running as fast as she could through the crowd.

There were tears streaking down her face as she ran toward the other bus stop. It's the doughnuts and chocolate, she told herself. That's why I'm crying. I didn't get to eat them. That's why I'm crying—

It was only after she had wormed her way onto the second bus that she remembered what the SP said: "Do you need help—?"

—And I ran away, she thought. I keep running away from people who are trying to help me. *Why?* Is it because I've been hiding and dodging so long that I can't stop?"

14

The Van Ness Avenue bus to Pacific Heights was much less crowded, and the few people on it were old, shabby, silent. They sat, as Til did, staring out through the grimy windows, indifferent to each other, and the packages on their laps were wrapped in wrinkled paper bags or newspaper tied with string. They looked as if they had been shopping in second-hand stores. Nearly all of the passengers were middle-aged or elderly people; Til had not seen another kid her age during the whole of her flight, except for one family of Chinese, whose children looked out calm and confident as lovely, cherished dolls from between their parents.

Til sat with her hands clenched in her lap, her feet braced against the bumps and lurches of the bus. At each bus stop they halted, and one of the ragged, shuffling passengers got off, another ragged, shuffling one got on. Street after street flashed by and even though they were on Van Ness Avenue, the sun had now set and the daylight seemed to fade faster the farther they got from Market Street.

Once again a bus ride was giving her time—whether she

wanted it or not—to think. Plunging through the crowds on Market Street, walking, running, dodging, kept your mind occupied, but the moment you found yourself sitting on that cold, greasy seat, with the dirty window beside you and the rumbling floor beneath your feet, everything you were trying not to think came flooding in:

What if I can't find Pop's apartment house? I've only been there once—I may not recognize it.

What if Pop isn't there? He told me he didn't spend any more time there than he could help.

If I can't find Pop, then what?

It was when she finally reached this point, this question, that Til acknowledged she had arrived at a dead end, the face of the cliff, the box canyon. The moment she had taken the money from the cup and run away was the moment of truth when she admitted that there was no longer any possibility of riding it out at home. She was utterly convinced that nothing now would stop Gertrude from killing her.

All of the crazy things that Gertrude had been doing for so long rose up before her now: the strange way she washed and scrubbed things that weren't dirty, as if she wanted to remove any sign of Til's presence in the house . . . the way she will wash and scrub up any marks . . . if I go back. Then there were Gertrude's long silences, the explosions of rage always directed at Til, the attacks that came out of nowhere, followed by periods of crazily calm, almost friendly, behavior. And always her refrain: "You think you're a *princess,* but I'm just a *slave,* a slave. Nobody cares about me. *Nobody cares about me.* "

Suddenly, like another of those optical illusions that she

saw during times of stress, the whole thing flopped over and she saw Gertrude from a completely different angle. It was true, what Gertrude said. Nobody cared about her.

Pop liked people who were funny and friendly, who liked to joke and talk. He backed away from people who were gloomy, troublesome, angry. Gertrude, on the other hand, lived at fever pitch, from crisis to crisis; she was constantly fearful and anxious, and she was endlessly trying to arouse sympathy and support from Pop. And the more she demanded, the less he gave.

Til couldn't remember a time when she could sense any warmth between Pop and her mother; she had grown up thinking this was the right and proper atmosphere between man and wife—one of ragged tempers, endless struggles to justify your own actions and put the other person down, insult, aggravation, accusation. Pop would come home and tell jokes and funny stories about his work, sing a song, play his violin, while Gertrude buzzed around like an angry bee, wanting to sting him (through his thick layers of fat) about the roof that leaked, the bill that was due, her tooth that ached. But he would always turn the stings aside with a joke.

And the more Pop joked, the angrier Gertrude became. If only . . . Til thought wistfully . . . if only Pop could have told fewer jokes, or Mom could have learned to tell more.

I did. Thinking back now, for the first time, Til realized suddenly that she had learned to imitate Pop, meet him on his own ground. Pop liked to keep the surface of things smooth, easy, comfortable, so she had learned to keep a smiling face when he was around. Together they made out like things were pretty good—it was like a circus act that they put on for each other, in which Gertrude did not play any part.

100

And nobody really cares about Mom. For a few minutes, watching the empty streets that branched off away from Van Ness like ribs on a skeleton, Til thought about Gertrude. It was true—she and Pop were warm and close, and nobody really cared much about Mom. Was that what made her this way—was that what had turned Gertrude so violent, so dangerous?

Suddenly Til realized that her head was aching again, and now all the bruises she had hidden, all the sprains she had concealed began to hurt too: the lumps on her head that she got when Gertrude pushed her down for rumpling her bedspread, leaving a ring in the bathtub, dropping her fork; the bruise on her ribs where Gertrude struck her with a broom handle for burning a piece of toast; the loose tooth that still wobbled in its socket after Gertrude hit her in the mouth for splashing water out of the dishpan.

"Pacific Avenue!" The bus driver's tired voice cut through to her. Til opened her eyes, buttoned her coat, picked up her lunch box and notebook, and stuffed the pencils into her pocket. As she stumbled to the front of the bus, the last piece of thought trickled through her mind: She can't hit Pop—he's too big. But I'm small; she *can* hit me. She can beat me. She can kill me—

—if I let her.

As the door of the bus hissed shut behind her, Til stared across Pacific Avenue. It was nearly deserted. The hill crested beyond Pacific Heights and the rows of lights ended abruptly where Van Ness Avenue began to drop down toward the marina and Fisherman's Wharf. Down the other slope, to the east, the streets ran to the brow of that hill and vanished again. Far beyond, although she could not see it from here, was the margin of the bay, and then on the other side of the water were the dimmed-out lights of Berkeley and Oakland, just beginning to glow now as dusk fell, like piles of diamonds in a Walt Disney movie. Overhead the sky was darkening and there was a trace of moisture in the air, as if it were about to start raining.

Til stood for a moment under the streetlight. The tin lunch box she had carried with her when she left the house (empty, of course) now banged against her side like a block of ice with a carrying handle. Suddenly, so late in the evening, she felt awkward and silly with it in her hand. Nobody in his right mind would be carrying a school lunch box at this hour. It would only make her more conspicuous, arouse suspicion, if a police patrol car might happen to cruise by. Across the sidewalk was the entrance of a tailor shop, closed for the night, and with a heavy chain fastened to a tub of purple pelargoniums. Til slid the lunch box and notebook in under the leaves of the flowers and stepped back.

She crossed Pacific Avenue, listening to the echo of her footsteps. It was like walking in a canyon in some unimaginably lost and distant wilderness. She could not see a single car or pedestrian in either direction, up or down the hill. If there had not been a few lights on in nearby windows, she would easily have believed that there was no one left on the planet besides herself.

On the other side of Pacific Avenue she turned left, crossed Van Ness, and started up the hill. Pop's building was in the next block, somewhere about the middle. Worst thing about it was that it was one of a set of twins—two buildings built with adjoining walls, with identical flights of stairs leading up (carved balusters, turned posts, gingerbread trim), two front porches with fan-lighted doors, bay windows shelving out over the sidewalk.

All I need now, thought Til, climbing the steep hill, is another drunk sailor. But the sailors, drunk or sober, stayed on Market Street and other downtown areas, where there were restaurants and movies and dance halls, so there wasn't much danger of another encounter like the one in the coffee shop.

Directly ahead of her now was the curved balustrade of the first of the twin buildings. A few feet more and she would have to decide which building to enter, and after that—

A rattle, soft and blurry, on her right. Til stopped, whirled around. Out of the shadows beneath a flight of steps emerged a black shape that shuffled forward, stopped, shuffled forward again. Til had just noticed that the shadow's head was uncovered (woman) and silver white (old) when the shadow reached out and laid a thin, cold hand on her arm.

Once again she opened her mouth and once again the scream would not come out. For three seconds they stood there—the silent, open-mouthed child and the silent, swaying old woman.

Then Til wrenched her arm clear and turned and ran. Without another thought she bolted up the first flight of stairs with the curved balustrade, yanked open the front door and slammed it behind her.

She leaned against the splintery old door as the scene before her seeped in past her blurry eyes and pounding heart: a dimly lit hallway directly ahead, carpeted with scraps of linoleum; a stairway to the left leading upward. The vestibule, if you could call it that, contained a rickety shelf, a cloudy

103

mirror, an umbrella stand empty except for some dusty cat-tails. All the walls were paneled in dark wood, and the tiny light bulb made the place look like a coal mine. But it *was* the right building, she was sure of that now.

Til turned her head and pressed her ear to the door, but heard nothing. Turned sideways, she saw a brass bolt on the door and quietly reached out and turned it. The door was now locked—and that would play hell with any tenant who came in during the next few minutes. But it would also keep the old woman—Til realized now that she was simply one of the street people—from following her.

Shouldn't have been so scared, she told herself as she started up the stairs. It was probably just old Sidewalk Sadie or one of the other derelicts who lived like rats—harmless, for the most part—on the streets of San Francisco. They ate out of garbage cans and slept in doorways, refusing like alley cats to be placed in charity homes, drifting around the city like dry leaves on the wind. All the same she was glad for the bolt on the door as she climbed the stairs.

She knew the number of Pop's apartment, but when she got there something stopped her. It looked different, although she could not tell exactly why. Perhaps there was a fraction of an inch less grime on the doorknob, a few less torn papers and cigarette butts around the door. Pop was not a neat person and the last thing in the world he would do was polish a doorknob.

She hesitated for several minutes but finally there was nothing else to do. She raised her fist to knock but even then stood there, hand in the air, for several seconds, before she struck the door. There was a moment's silence and then the sound of heavy footsteps. One more minute and it would be over—

The door opened.

But it wasn't Pop.

It was the street photographer—the big, blonde, fat woman who had taken Til's picture on Market Street with Pop.

Til stared up at the woman, and the whole world crashed down around her. She had counted so much on seeing Pop here that all her brittle plans exploded, and she had no strength to fall back on, to make new plans. She was exhausted with the effort it had cost her just to get here, and suddenly it seemed that the last exit from hell was barred by a big woman who was still wearing the straw hat with the cards and memo pad in it.

For the space of a second Til and the woman stared at each other. Then, mechanically, Til turned to run. She had come to find Pop and he was not there. She was too tired—it was too black inside her head—for her to try to change directions now. If she hadn't been able to talk to Mrs. Hoogendorn or the school nurse, what could she possibly say to this stranger with the queer hat?

She did not look back as she fled downstairs, did not see the blonde woman reach out to her, did not hear her cry: "Til! Wait—is something—? Wait—Til—*wait*—"

It took only a few seconds to roll the bolt back, open the door, vault over the balustrade, race down the sidewalk toward Van Ness. The bus—yes, there it was like a square box of light. As it slid to a stop, the door hissed open and Til sprang in, threw her dime into the hopper. It did not occur to her to do anything else. This was the only bus route—besides the one to Playland and the one on Third Street—that she knew. Her life had been bounded by Pacific Heights on one end and Quesada Avenue on the other; all she could do was ricochet between the two perimeters until something—or somebody—stopped her—

She did not look back at all. She did not see the big blonde woman, hampered by weight and clumsy without her shoes on, who galloped down the stairs of the apartment building and out onto the street seconds after the bus disappeared up the hill on Van Ness.

Nor did she see Sidewalk Sadie, who emerged from some black corner and bobbed up to the photographer, raising her bony arms to describe how a little girl had come running out of the apartment house, jumped off the porch, and ran down the street to board the bus—

Helga stared after the bus as it disappeared up Van Ness Avenue. She cursed herself for being so fat, so slow—but the child ran like a deer. Who could possibly keep up with her?

Sidewalk Sadie had faded back into the shadows as Helga turned and climbed the hill back to the apartment house as fast as she could. The cold pavement was like ice under her stockinged feet, and she was out of breath and shaking with a chill by the time she slammed the door to Helmut's apartment behind her.

She leaned against the door for a moment and tried to think. Alarms were clanging through her mind like fire engines roaring up the Powell Street hill. Til—she had recognized her instantly, of course—Til must be in terrible trouble to have come all this way hoping to see her father at this time of night. Trouble—what was that in Helmut's note—

106

something about Til and trouble? She grabbed up the note, read it again, threw it down.

The only thing clear about it all was that she would have to try to help Til. Shoes—yes, there they were on the floor where she had kicked them off. Glancing longingly at the cold coffeepot—she literally ached to rest awhile and have a cup of hot coffee—Helga pulled on her shoes, tied a bandana over her head, checked to make sure she had some money in her purse.

She had known from the instant when Til turned and started to run that she would have to follow her. She could not possibly ignore the terrible plea for help, the fear and desperation she had seen on Til's face in that split second. The only real question was: Should she take time to call Helmut? If Til was out on the street—a most dangerous place for a child to be at this hour—it could only be because something had gone terribly wrong at home. But she, Helga, had no authority to deal with that situation. She would follow Til, try to watch over her, but it would need Helmut to handle whatever was happening at the house on Quesada Avenue.

Quickly she called the number that Helmut had left for her in case of emergencies. The voice at the other end was harsh and distracted. "Hello? Hello?"

"Hello. You must help me. It is an emergency—"

"Hello?"

"Emergency—" When Helga got nervous her accent got thicker. She had never minded it till now; it was just something—being German-born and speaking with an accent—that she had shared with Helmut. Now she tried hard to sound American, so the voice at the other end of the line would respond.

"E-mer-gency," she said carefully. "Please—call Helmut Foerester. Tell him—"

"Yeah? Yeah? Hurry up, lady, I got a ship to load here—"

"Tell him—his daughter—in trouble. Very bad. Tell him—to go to Quesada Avenue—"

"Where's that? Quesada?"

"Yah. Yes. Quesada Avenue. He knows. Tell him—to *hurry*—"

Oh, mein Gott, she thought as she heard the harsh voice say "Okay, okay, lady—" and the phone at the other end went back on the hook. *Oh, mein Gott*—what if they don't tell him?

But there was no more time to think about that. Locking the apartment door behind her, Helga dropped the key in her pocket, let herself out, and hurried down the hill to catch the Van Ness Avenue bus. If only the next bus wasn't late—

Til never remembered either of the bus rides home. She must have gotten off the Van Ness Avenue bus on Market Street, walked down to Third Street and climbed on the Third Street bus, but she was unable to remember any of it. It was like being in a deep sleep, and she only began to wake up again as the bus slid to a halt at the foot of the Quesada Avenue hill.

What am I doing here? she thought. I'm not supposed to be out riding around on a bus in the middle of the night. Why did I run away? Something about a Ferris wheel—

Silly. There aren't any Ferris wheels on Quesada Avenue—

She stood at the bottom of the hill for a long time in a pool of shadow at the entrance to an alley. As the hour grew later, traffic and movement of any kind in the streets lessened, and the city noises seemed muted and far distant. She was very cold and now for some reason she began to worry about what she had done with her lunch box. She was sure she had it with her when she left the house—whenever that had been. Mom will really get me for this, she told herself. The last time I lost a lunch box, she whipped me till my backside was bleeding—

She was aware, as she started up the hill, that ever since she had failed to find Pop, she was only thinking with a very small piece of her mind. All the rest of it had been blacked out, like the buildings with heavy curtains over the windows to cut out light during air raid drills. Things were probably still happening behind those curtains, but you couldn't see because of the blackout. But maybe there wasn't anything left behind the black curtains in her mind. Maybe all there was now for her was this little lighted place. . . .

As she came abreast of the split in the street, by force of long habit, she crossed the lower street and started to climb the steep bank where the trees and bushes grew. The two sections of the street above and below her were fairly well lit by the lights at each end of the block, but it was almost completely dark where she stood. Most of the houses in the neighborhood were now dark and quiet, with only a window here and there that showed a little light from behind drawn shades.

Her own house was completely dark. That was odd, she thought. Gertrude generally kept a light on—sometimes, of late, all night. If Til woke during the night, she could not tell what time it was because the house would still be light.

109

But now it was dark. Puzzled, Til leaned back farther into the shadows. She was still trying to remember where she had left her lunch box, and why she was out here on the street at night instead of in bed. And most of all—what day it was. Or what day it would be as soon as morning broke. Would it be Friday, a day when she would go to school? Or would it be Saturday—the day when she would ride the Ferris wheel—

At the thought of the Ferris wheel and the way the Ferris wheel seized her like some great, obscene, stinking monster and swung her around and around, bruising and hurting and trying to kill her—she started. Unconsciously she stepped forward into the light. And, as Til stepped forward, so did Gertrude.

Gertrude had been standing in the shadow of the porch, waiting. And in her hand, Til could see the knife.

I ought to run, she told herself.

But this is my *mother*—

I must run—

But she had already run. She had run clear to Pacific Heights—to Pop—and he wasn't there. Just the fat lady with the strange hat, and Sidewalk Sadie, and a dingy, empty apartment house.

No, there is no use to run now. No place to run to.

Gertrude raised a hand, the one without the knife, and beckoned to her. Til took one step, another. The lighted place in her head was getting very small; she had almost no place left to think.

Gertrude stepped forward and began to descend the steps, silently, without creaking a single board. She beckoned again.

110

Til sighed. She was trying to push back the blackout in her head and think—think—this is my mother—but there was something about the Ferris wheel—oh, it was so dark, there by the Ferris wheel—

The hand Gertrude stretched out to her, fingers spread to grasp, was shaking, and the other, slightly back and up in the shadows, held the knife raised to strike.

Oh, so dark *so dark* now—

No! It wasn't dark! All at once it was very bright. Lights had suddenly appeared all around, and Til and Gertrude were standing as if on center stage, outlined in the blaze. And the light came from headlights—the headlights of a police patrol car that had appeared out of nowhere.

Gertrude's hand flicked once, turned the knife under so that it lay concealed beneath her arm and wrist. Behind Til, car doors clicked open and shut, and two huge men in uniform, carrying brilliant flashlights that blinded her, closed in on either side. The patrol car's engine purred softly, and in the beams from the headlights the first ticking drops of rain showed like silver dotted lines.

Til stood silent, frozen.

"Good evening, ma'am," said one of the officers politely to Gertrude. "I'm Sergeant Polaski, police department. We received a call from a Helmut Foerester—I understand that you might be having a little trouble here?"

Gertrude blinked, shivered slightly. Then, apparently, dazed, upset, she reached out as if to grab Til, to get her hands on an exasperating child who needed to be taken back into the house where she would be safe—

"Trouble?" said Gertrude. Then she nodded. "Yes—but I am going to put a stop to it. I know how to stop this trouble.

111

Til—she''—nodding toward Til who still stood between the officers—''she ran away. A bad girl! But now she's back—yes, I will put a stop to this trouble now, officer. It is—all over now. Just—I'll just take her inside—''

And kill me, thought Til. It won't matter to her now whether or not she covers up the mess or anybody finds out, because she doesn't care anymore. She won't bother to hide the marks because she's too crazy to care. It's gone beyond hiding now. But I'm the only one who knows it—I'm the only one who knows about how she hates me—about the beatings—about the knives—

Gertrude smiled and nodded at the policeman. "Bad, bad girl," she chided gently, almost with affection. "But I can handle the trouble now. I know just what to do with this little girl. She thinks she's a princess, and I'm just a slave—''

Til took a deep breath. In a minute it'll be too late—I have to make her do something so they'll *see*—nobody will believe me if I just tell them she's going to kill me. I've got to do something—I've got to make *her* do something so they'll see for themselves that she's going to kill me—this is the only chance I have left—

"Slave!" Til screamed. "Slave! I'm a princess and you're just an ugly old slave! Nobody cares about *you*—''

Gertrude's head snapped up. She sucked in a deep rasping breath. Like a flash of cruel light the knife appeared in her hand. With a cry of utmost rage she sprang across the sidewalk at Til, knife raised, and when it came down, stopped by the policeman's hand, the blade just knicked the skin of his wrist, but Til's neck was unmarked.

15

Til sat in the back seat of the police car, wedged in between the blonde photographer, Helga, who had an arm around her, and an elderly policeman on the other who was writing something in a notebook. Til could see Pop (when did he and Helga get here?) as he walked back and forth from time to time across the headlights of the police car. He watched, sick-faced and silent, as some white-uniformed men quietly but forcefully put Gertrude into the ambulance.

After the policeman had seized the knife, Gertrude had started to scream. For several minutes, the sound covered everything that was happening on the street, including the sound of a rattly old blue Chevrolet that churned up the Quesada Avenue hill, choked out, was started again, and came to an awkward halt just behind the police car. Through the haze of sickness and terror that had gripped her, Til became aware of Mrs. Hoogendorn, followed by Mrs. Foley (now in a baggy tweed dress and so nearly unrecognizable) as they climbed out of the Chevrolet and struggled the rest of the way up the hill.

"Clotilde!" gasped Mrs. Hoogendorn. "Oh, my dear

113

child! What has hap—— Are you all right?'' She reached out her warm, friendly arms, and the very next layer of arms, like the second blanket on a cold night, were those of the school nurse. Released in a moment, Til stood blinking and hiccoughing up at the two women.

''Hours!'' cried Mrs. Hoogendorn, fanning her face, which was flushed in spite of the cold. ''It took us *hours* to borrow some gas—I'd used up almost all my gas rationing stamps—and then my old car—it wouldn't start—and it stalled on Third Street—oh, Clotilde, we were so worried! Mrs. Foley told me you came to see her—tried to talk to her—and we just *had* to come and see if we could help you. We have been so *frantic*—''

So was *I,* thought Til dully. She nodded, feeling a strange slackness come over her now as she stared at the crowd around her. When had they all come? She did not really know, or care. After a hideous night of lonely bus rides, and hands that grabbed her, and shadows, and knives, she knew there could never be too many people around her now.

After talking to Pop and to the police. Mrs. Hoogendorn and the school nurse, satisfied that Til was safe now at last, had kissed her and climbed back into their own car. They backed down to the end of the center strip, turned, and started down the hill. The Chevrolet was still bucking and backfiring as its taillights winked out around the corner.

Now Til huddled down on the back seat of the police car, her head bent, trying not to watch as Gertrude fought the policemen and ambulance attendants. Her voice, screaming curses, was not a human voice—it sounded like the desperate bellowing of an animal caught in a trap.

Tears streamed down Til's face. I'm crying, she thought.

Crying for someone who beat me—kicked me—tried to kill me—

"Crying," said the big blonde woman. Her arm around Til was as warm and pillowy as a comforter. From her pocket she took a man's handkerchief—Til instantly recognized it as one of Pop's—and mopped Til's face. "It is a time for crying."

Til raised her head. Shaking, she stared around at all of them—Helga, the police, Pop, the ambulance crew. "I don't—understand—" she whispered.

Pop leaned through the open door of the patrol car and reached out his hand to smooth it over Til's head. She saw with shock and disbelief that Pop was crying too. "Yah," he said softly, "it *is* a time for crying—" He pulled out another handkerchief from his pocket and blew his nose.

"You know—" Til was so tired, but she felt she had to get it all out now. After all, they *said* it was the time for crying— "You know, she always said—she was a *slave*—that nobody cared about her—" Til paused and Pop nodded, sighed.

"Is it—did *we*—make her this way? Maybe—if we had cared more about her—because—well, we *didn't,* you know—but would she have been—different—if we *had* cared more—Pop?"

The elderly policeman, finished with his note-taking, crawled out of the patrol car. At a gesture from him, Pop slowly and wearily climbed in and the three of them, Helga, Til and Pop, were now enclosed in a warm, quiet place together and alone. Some of the noise and bright lights were gone now. The ambulance, its doors locked, was halfway down the hill; Til noticed that it did not have its sirens blow-

115

ing. She supposed it was because there was now no need to hurry . . . for Gertrude.

"No . . ." said Pop at last. "I don't . . . really think the way your mother acted had much to do with us. No—you musn't spend the rest of your life blaming yourself, Til. You see—there are some people—like your mother—for them, there is *never* enough. Never enough money. Never enough happiness. Never enough safety or comfort or love— especially love. They always need more. It's like they have holes in them and all the good things you give them just run out and are wasted, and they want more all the time. And then they start to blame others, like you, calling you a princess, because they are so unhappy. They blame and they blame until finally—" Pop's plump hand made a weary gesture at the now dark and empty street, the dark and empty house. "No, Til"—Pop sighed and rubbed his forehead tiredly—"if you want to blame somebody, *I* am the one. I never should have left you—"

"Helmut, the court gave Til to her mother," said Helga quietly. It was almost the first time she had spoken.

"Yes, I know . . . but—I was wrong. I didn't realize—I should have asked more questions—found out what was going on—"

"Pop—no—"

"Yes. It's true. There will always be fault for me here. I wanted to believe that everything was all right, so I did. I didn't look. I didn't listen. I turned away—"

One of the policemen, who had earlier told them he would take them back to Helmut's apartment in Pacific Heights, opened the door of the squad car and slid behind the wheel. He stepped on the starter, backed down and around the center

116

strip, and the patrol car turned and slid away down the Quesada Avenue hill.

Til sighed and nodded as the houses on the steep hill vanished behind her into the darkness. We're all at fault, she thought to herself. I tried not to believe what my eyes saw and my ears heard because I didn't want to believe it. Well, I've learned my lesson. Up *is* up. Black *is* black and white *is* white, and you've got to be able to tell the difference between what you see . . . and what you want to see.

My mother *did* hate me. She *did* try to kill me. And *I* was the only one who could stop her. If I hadn't screamed at her when I did—

She thought for a brief moment about the knife and how it had gleamed in the headlights of the patrol car. And *I* stopped her, Til told herself. I stopped the knife. All those people there—Pop, Mrs. Hoogendorn, Mrs. Foley, the police—couldn't do anything until *I* stopped her by yelling and making them see what she was really like, what she was going to do to me. So I guess . . . *sometimes* you've got to save yourself . . . by yourself.

And now at last she knew something else too. Til knew that she would never—for the rest of her life—ride on the Ferris wheel again.